Doris Lessing was born of Britis[...]  in 1919 and was taken to South[...] when she was five. She spent her [...] and first came to England in 1[...] manuscript of her first novel, 7[...] published in 1950 with outstandi[...] ica, and in ten European countries. Since then her international reputation not only as a novelist, but as a non-fiction and short-story writer has flourished. For her collection of short novels, *Five*, she was honoured with the Somerset Maugham Award. She was awarded the Austrian State Prize for European Literature in 1981, and the German Federal Republic Shakespeare Prize of 1982. Among her other celebrated novels are the five-volume *Children of Violence* series, *The Golden Notebook*, *The Summer Before the Dark* and *Memoirs of a Survivor*. Many of her short stories have been collected in two volumes entitled *To Room Nineteen* and *The Temptation of Jack Orkney*, while her African stories appear in *This Was the Old Chief's Country* and *The Sun Between Their Feet*. *Shikasta*, the first in the series of five novels with the overall title of *Canopus in Argos: Archives*, was published in 1979. Her novel *The Good Terrorist* won the W. H. Smith Literary Award for 1985.

By the same author

DORIS LESSING

The Black Madonna

Paladin
An Imprint of HarperCollins*Publishers*

Paladin
An Imprint of HarperCollins*Publishers*
77–85 Fulham Palace Road,
Hammersmith, London W6 8JB

Published by Paladin 1992
9 8 7 6 5 4 3 2 1

Previously published by GraftonBooks 1966
Reprinted eight times

First published in Great Britain by
Michael Joseph Ltd as part of the collection
African Stories, 1964

This selection copyright © Doris Lessing 1966

The Author asserts the moral right to
be identified as the author of this work

ISBN 0 586 09111 4

Set in Baskerville

Printed in Great Britain by
HarperCollinsManufacturing Glasgow

Contents

The Black Madonna

There are some countries in which the arts, let alone Art, cannot be said to flourish. Why this should be so it is hard to say, although of course we all have our theories about it. For sometimes it is the most barren soil that sends up gardens of those flowers which we all agree are the crown and justification of life, and it is this fact which makes it hard to say, finally, why the soil of Zambesia should produce such reluctant plants.

Zambesia is a rough, sunburnt, virile, positive country contemptuous of subtleties and sensibility; yet there have been States with these qualities which have produced art, though perhaps with the left hand. Zambesia is, to put it mildly, unsympathetic to those ideas so long taken for granted in other parts of the world, to do with liberty, fraternity and the rest. Yet there are those, and some of the finest souls among them, who maintain that art is impossible without a minority whose leisure is guaranteed by a hard-working majority. And whatever Zambesia's comfortable minority may lack, it is not leisure.

Zambesia – but enough; out of respect for ourselves and for scientific accuracy, we should refrain from jumping to conclusions. Particularly when one remembers the almost wistful respect Zambesians show when an artist does appear in their midst.

Consider, for instance, the case of Michele.

He came out of the internment camp at the time when Italy was made a sort of honorary ally, during the Second World War. It was a time of strain for the authorities, because it is one thing to be responsible for thousands of prisoners of war whom one must treat according to certain recognized standards; it is another to be faced, and from one day to the next, with these same thousands transformed by some international legerdemain into comrades in arms. Some of the thousands stayed where they were in the camps; they were fed and housed there at least. Others went as farm labourers, though not many; for while the farmers were as always short of labour, they did not know how to handle farm labourers who were also white men: such a phenomenon had never happened in Zambesia before. Some did odd jobs around the towns, keeping a sharp eye out for the trade unions, who would neither admit them as members nor agree to their working.

Hard, hard, the lot of these men, but fortunately not for long, for soon the war ended and they were able to go home.

Hard, too, the lot of the authorities, as has been pointed out; and for that reason they were doubly willing to take what advantages they could from the situation; and that Michele was such an advantage there could be no doubt.

His talents were first discovered when he was still a prisoner of war. A church was built in the camp, and Michele decorated its interior. It became a show-place, that little tin-roofed church in the prisoners' camp, with its whitewashed walls covered all over with frescoes depicting swarthy peasants gathering grapes from the vintage, beautiful Italian girls dancing, plump dark-eyed children. Amid crowded scenes of Italian life appeared the Virgin and her Child, smiling and beneficent, happy to move familiarly among her people.

Culture-loving ladies who had bribed the authorities to be taken inside the camp would say, 'Poor thing, how homesick he must be.' And they would beg to be allowed to leave half a crown for the artist. Some were indignant. He was a prisoner, after all, captured in the very act of fighting against justice and democracy, and what right had he to protest? – for they felt these paintings as a sort of protest. What was there in Italy that we did not have right here in Westonville, which was the capital and hub of Zambesia? Were there not sunshine and mountains and fat babies and pretty girls here? Did we not grow – if not grapes, at least lemons and oranges and flowers in plenty?

People were upset – the desperation of nostalgia came from the painted white walls of that simple church, and affected everyone according to their temperament.

But when Michele was free, his talent was remembered. He

was spoken of as 'that Italian artist'. As a matter of fact, he was a brick-layer. And the virtues of those frescoes might very well have been exaggerated. It is possible they would have been overlooked altogether in a country where picture-covered walls were more common.

When one of the visiting ladies came rushing out to the camp in her own car, to ask him to paint her children, he said he was not qualified to do so. But at last he agreed. He took a room in the town and made some nice likenesses of the children. Then he painted the children of a great number of the first lady's friends. He charged ten shillings a time. Then one of the ladies wanted a portrait of herself. He asked ten pounds for it; it had taken him a month to do. She was annoyed, but paid.

And Michele went off to his room with a friend and stayed there drinking red wine from the Cape and talking about home. While the money lasted he could not be persuaded to do any more portraits.

There was a good deal of talk among the ladies about the dignity of labour, a subject in which they were well versed, and one felt they might almost go so far as to compare a white man with a kaffir, who did not understand the dignity of labour either.

He was felt to lack gratitude. One of the ladies tracked him down, found him lying on a camp-bed under a tree with a bottle of wine, and spoke to him severely about the barbarity of Mussolini and the fecklessness of the Italian temperament. Then she demanded that he should instantly paint a picture of herself in her new evening dress. He refused, and she went home very angry.

It happened that she was the wife of one of our most important citizens, a General or something of that kind, who was at that time engaged in planning a military tattoo or show for the benefit of the civilian population. The whole of Westonville had been discussing this show for weeks. We were all bored to extinction by dances, fancy-dress balls, fairs, lotteries and other charitable entertainments. It is not too much to say that while some were dying for freedom, others were dancing for it. There comes a limit to everything. Though, of course, when the end of the war actually came and the thousands of troops stationed in the country had to go home – in short, when enjoying ourselves would no longer be a duty, many were heard to exclaim that life would never be the same again.

In the meantime, the Tattoo would make a nice change for us all. The military gentlemen responsible for the idea did not think of it in these terms. They thought to improve morale by giving us some idea of what war was really like. Headlines in the newspaper were not enough. And in order to bring it all home to us, they planned to destroy a village by shell-fire before our very eyes.

First, the village had to be built.

It appears that the General and his subordinates stood around in the red dust of the parade-ground under a burning sun for the whole of one day, surrounded by building materials, while hordes of African labourers ran around with boards and nails, trying to make something that looked like a village. It became evident that they would have to build a proper village in order to destroy it; and this would cost more than was allowed for the whole entertainment. The General went home in a bad temper, and his wife said what they needed was an artist, they needed Michele. This was not because she wanted to do Michele a good turn; she could not endure the thought of him lying around singing while there was work to be done. She refused to undertake any delicate diplomatic missions when her husband said he would be damned if he would ask favours of any little Wop. She solved the problem for him in her own way: a certain Captain Stocker was sent out to fetch him.

The Captain found him on the same camp-bed under the same tree, in rolled-up trousers, an uncollared shirt, unshaven, mildly drunk, with a bottle of wine standing beside him on the earth. He was singing an air so wild, so sad, that the Captain was uneasy. He stood at ten paces from the disreputable fellow and felt the indignities of his position. A year ago, this man had been a mortal enemy to be shot at sight. Six months ago, he had been an enemy prisoner. Now he lay with his knees up, in an untidy shirt that had certainly once been military. For the Captain, the situation crystallized in a desire that Michele should salute him.

'Piselli!' he said sharply.

Michele turned his head and looked at the Captain from the horizontal. 'Good morning,' he said affably.

'You are wanted,' said the Captain.

'Who?' said Michele. He sat up, a fattish, olive-skinned little man. His eyes were resentful.

'The authorities.'

'The war is over?'

The Captain, who was already stiff and shiny enough in his laundered khaki, jerked his head back frowning, chin out. He was a large man, blond, and wherever his flesh showed, it was brick-red. His eyes were small and blue and angry. His red hands, covered all over with fine yellow bristles, clenched by his side. Then he saw the disappointment in Michele's eyes, and they unclenched. 'No, it is not over,' he said. 'Your assistance is required.'

'For the war?'

'For the war effort. I take it you are interested in defeating the Germans?'

Michele looked at the Captain. The little dark-eyed artisan looked at the great blond officer with his cold blue eyes, his narrow mouth, his hands like bristle-covered steaks. He looked and said: 'I am very interested in the end of the war.'

'*Well?*' said the Captain between his teeth.

'The pay?' said Michele.

'You will be paid.'

Michele stood up. He lifted the bottle against the sun, then took a gulp. He rinsed his mouth out with wine and spat. Then he poured what was left on to the red earth, where it made a bubbling purple stain.

'I am ready,' he said. He went with the Captain to the waiting lorry, where he climbed in beside the driver's seat and not, as the Captain had expected, into the back of the lorry. When they had arrived at the parade-ground the officers had left a message that the Captain would be personally responsible for Michele and for the village. Also for the hundred or so labourers who were sitting around on the grass verges waiting for orders.

The Captain explained what was wanted. Michele nodded. Then he waved his hands at the Africans. 'I do not want these,' he said.

'You will do it yourself – a village?'

'Yes.'

'With no help?'

Michele smiled for the first time. 'I will do it.'

The Captain hesitated. He disapproved on principle of white men doing heavy manual labour. He said: 'I will keep six to do the heavy work.'

Michele shrugged; and the Captain went over and dismissed all but six of the Africans. He came back with them to Michele.

'It is hot,' said Michele.

'Very,' said the Captain. They were standing in the middle of the parade-ground. Around its edge trees, grass, gulfs of shadow. Here, nothing but ṛeddish dust, drifting and lifting in a low hot breeze.

'I am thirsty,' said Michele. He grinned. The Captain felt his stiff lips loosen unwillingly in reply. The two pairs of eyes met. It was a moment of understanding. For the Captain, the little Italian had suddenly become human. 'I will arrange it,' he said, and went off down-town. By the time he had explained the position to the right people, filled in forms and made arrangements, it was late afternoon. He returned to the parade-ground with a case of Cape brandy, to find Michele and the six black men seated together under a tree. Michele was singing an Italian song to them, and they were harmonizing with him. The sight affected the Captain like an attack of nausea. He came up, and the Africans stood to attention. Michele continued to sit.

'You said you would do the work yourself?'

'Yes, I said so.'

The Captain then dismissed the Africans. They departed, with friendly looks towards Michele, who waved at them. The Captain was beef-red with anger. 'You have not started yet?'

'How long have I?'

'Three weeks.'

'Then there is plenty of time,' said Michele, looking at the bottle of brandy in the Captain's hand. In the other were two glasses. 'It is evening,' he pointed out. The Captain stood frowning for a moment. Then he sat down on the grass, and poured out two brandies.

'Ciao,' said Michele.

'Cheers,' said the Captain. Three weeks, he was thinking. Three weeks with this damned little Itie! He drained his glass

and refilled it, and set it in the grass. The grass was cool and
soft. A tree was flowering somewhere close – hot waves of
perfume came on the breeze.

'It is nice here,' said Michele. 'We will have a good time
together. Even in a war, there are times of happiness. And of
friendship. I drink to the end of the war.'

Next day, the Captain did not arrive at the parade-ground
until after lunch. He found Michele under the trees with a bottle.
Sheets of ceiling board had been erected at one end of the parade-
grond in such a way that they formed two walls and part of a
third, and a slant of steep roof supported on struts.

'What's that?' said the Captain, furious.

'The church,' said Michele.

'Wha-at?'

'You will see. Later. It is very hot.' He looked at the brandy
bottle that lay on its side on the ground. The Captain went to
the lorry and returned with the case of brandy. They drank.
Time passed. It was a long time since the Captain had sat on
grass under a tree. It was a long time, for that matter, since he
had drunk so much. He always drank a great deal, but it was
regulated to the times and seasons. He was a disciplined man.
Here, sitting on the grass beside this little man whom he still
could not help thinking of as an enemy, it was not that he let his
self-discipline go, but that he felt himself to be something
different: he was temporarily set outside his normal behaviour.
Michele did not count. He listened to Michele talking about
Italy, and it seemed to him he was listening to a savage speaking:
as if he heard tales from the mythical South Sea islands where a
man like himself might very well go just once in his life. He found
himself saying he would like to make a trip to Italy after the war.
Actually, he was attracted only by the North and by Northern
people. He had visited Germany, under Hitler, and though it
was not the time to say so, he found it very satisfactory. Then
Michele sang him some Italian songs. He sang Michele some
English ones. Then Michele took out photographs of his wife and
children, who lived in a village in the mountains of North Italy.
He asked the Captain if he were married. The Captain never
spoke about his private affairs.

He had spent all his life in one or other of the African colonies

as a policeman, magistrate, native commissioner, or in some
other useful capacity. When the war started, military life came
easily to him. But he hated city life, and had his own reasons for
wishing the war was over. Mostly, he had been in bush-stations
with one or two other white men, or by himself, far from the
rigours of civilization. He had relations with native women; and
from time to time visited the city where his wife lived with her
parents and the children. He was always tormented by the idea
that she was unfaithful to him. Recently he had even appointed
a private detective to watch her; he was convinced the detective
was inefficient. Army friends coming from L—where his wife
was, spoke of her at parties, enjoying herself. When the war
ended, she would not find it so easy to have a good time. And
why did he not simply live with her and be done with it? The
fact was, he could not. And his long exile to remote bush-stations
was because he needed the excuse not to. He could not bear to
think of his wife for too long; she was that part of his life he had
never been able, so to speak, to bring to heel.

Yet he spoke of her now to Michele, and of his favourite bush-
wife, Nadya. He told Michele the story of his life, until he
realized that the shadows from the trees they sat under had
stretched right across the parade-ground to the grandstand. He
got unsteadily to his feet, and said: 'There is work to be done.
You are being paid to work.'

'I will show you my church when the light goes.'

The sun dropped, darkness fell, and Michele made the Captain
drive his lorry on to the parade-ground a couple of hundred
yards away and switch on his lights. Instantly, a white church
sprang up from the shapes and shadows of the bits of board.

'Tomorrow, some houses,' said Michele cheerfully.

At the end of a week, the space at the end of the parade-
ground had crazy gawky constructions of lath and board over it,
that looked in the sunlight like nothing on this earth. Privately,
it upset the Captain; it was like a nightmare that these skeleton-
like shapes should be able to persuade him, with the illusions of
light and dark, that they were a village. At night, the Captain
drove up his lorry, switched on the lights, and there it was, the
village, solid and real against a background of full green trees.

Then, in the morning sunlight, there was nothing there, just bits of board stuck in the sand.

'It is finished,' said Michele.

'You were engaged for three weeks,' said the Captain. He did not want it to end, this holiday from himself.

Michele shrugged. 'The army is rich,' he said. Now, to avoid curious eyes, they sat inside the shade of the church, with the case of brandy between them. The Captain talked, talked endlessly, about his wife, about women. He could not stop talking.

Michele listened. Once he said: 'When I go home – when I go home – I shall open my arms . . .' He opened them, wide. He closed his eyes. Tears ran down his cheeks. 'I shall take my wife in my arms, and I shall ask nothing, nothing. I do not care. It is enough to be together. That is what the war has taught me. It is enough, it is enough. I shall ask no questions and I shall be happy.'

The Captain stared before him, suffering. He thought how he dreaded his wife. She was a scornful creature, gay and hard, who laughed at him. She had been laughing at him since they married. Since the war, she had taken to calling him names like Little Hitler, and Storm-trooper. 'Go ahead, my little Hitler,' she had cried last time they met. 'Go ahead, my Storm-trooper. If you want to waste your money on private detectives, go ahead. But don't think I don't know what *you* do when you're in the bush. I don't care what you do, but remember that I know it . . .'

The Captain remembered her saying it. And there sat Michele on his packing-case, saying: 'It's a pleasure for the rich, my friend, detectives and the law. Even jealousy is a pleasure I don't want any more. Ah, my friend, to be together with my wife again, and the children, that is all I ask of life. That and wine and food and singing in the evenings.' And the tears wetted his cheeks and splashed on to his shirt.

That a man should cry, good lord! thought the Captain. And without shame! He seized the bottle and drank.

Three days before the great occasion, some high-ranking officers came strolling through the dust, and found Michele and the Captain sitting together on the packing-case, singing. The Captain's shirt was open down the front, and there were stains on it.

The Captain stood to attention with the bottle in his hand, and Michele stood to attention too, out of sympathy with his friend. Then the officers drew the Captain aside – they were all cronies of his – and said, what the hell did he think he was doing? And why wasn't the village finished?

Then they went away.

'Tell them it is finished,' said Michele. 'Tell them I want to go.'

'No,' said the Captain, 'no. Michele, what would you do if your wife . . .'

'This world is a good place. We should be happy – that is all.'

'Michele . . .'

'I want to go. There is nothing to do. They paid me yesterday.'

'Sit down, Michele. Three more days, and then it's finished.'

'Then I shall paint the inside of the church as I painted the one in the camp.'

The Captain laid himself down on some boards and went to sleep. When he woke, Michele was surrounded by the pots of paint he had used on the outside of the village. Just in front of the Captain was a picture of a black girl. She was young and plump. She wore a patterned blue dress and her shoulders came soft and bare out of it. On her back was a baby slung in a band of red stuff. Her face was turned towards the Captain and she was smiling.

'That's Nadya,' said the Captain. 'Nadya . . .' He groaned loudly. He looked at the black child and shut his eyes. He opened them, and mother and child were still there. Michele was very carefully drawing thin yellow circles around the heads of the black girl and her child.

'Good God,' said the Captain, 'you can't do that.'

'Why not?'

'You can't have a black Madonna.'

'She was a peasant. This is a peasant. Black peasant Madonna for black country.'

'This is a German village,' said the Captain.

'This is my Madonna,' said Michele angrily. 'Your German village and my Madonna. I paint this picture as an offering to the Madonna. She is pleased – I feel it.'

The Captain lay down again. He was feeling ill. He went back to sleep. When he woke for the second time it was dark. Michele had brought in a flaring paraffin lamp, and by its light was working on the long wall. A bottle of brandy stood beside him. He painted until long after midnight, and the Captain lay on his side and watched, as passive as a man suffering a dream. Then they both went to sleep on the boards. The whole of the next day Michele stood painting black Madonnas, black saints, black angels. Outside, troops were practising in the sunlight, bands were blaring and motor cyclists roared up and down. But Michele painted on, drunk and oblivious. The Captain lay on his back, drinking and muttering about his wife. Then he would say 'Nadya, Nadya', and burst into sobs.

Towards nightfall the troops went away. The officers came back, and the Captain went off with them to show how the village sprang into being when the great lights at the end of the parade-ground were switched on. They all looked at the village in silence. They switched the lights off, and there were only the tall angular boards leaning like gravestones in the moonlight. On went the lights – and there was the village. They were silent, as if suspicious. Like the Captain, they seemed to feel it was not right. Uncanny it certainly was, but *that* was not it. Unfair – that was the word. It was cheating. And profoundly disturbing.

'Clever chap, that Italian of yours,' said the General.

The Captain, who had been woodenly correct until this moment, suddenly came rocking up to the General, and steadied himself by laying his hand on the august shoulder. 'Bloody Wops,' he said. 'Bloody kaffirs. Bloody ... Tell you what, though, there's one Itie that's some good. Yes, there is, I'm telling you. He's a friend of mine, actually.'

The General looked at him. Then he nodded at his underlings. The Captain was taken away for disciplinary purposes. It was decided, however, that he must be ill, nothing else could account for such behaviour. He was put to bed in his own room with a nurse to watch him.

He woke twenty-four hours later, sober for the first time in weeks. He slowly remembered what had happened. Then he sprang out of bed and rushed into his clothes. The nurse was just in time to see him run down the path and leap into his car.

He drove at top speed to the parade-ground, which was flooded

with light in such a way that the village did not exist. Everything
was in full swing. The cars were three deep around the square
with people on the running-boards and even the roofs. The
grandstand was packed. Women dressed up as gipsies, country
girls, Elizabethan court dames, and so on, wandered about with
trays of ginger beer and sausage-rolls and programmes at five
shillings each in aid of the war effort. On the square, troops
deployed, obsolete machine-guns were being dragged up and
down, bands played, and motor cyclists roared through flames.

As the Captain parked the lorry, all this activity ceased, and
the lights went out. The Captain began running around the
outside of the square to reach the place where the guns were
hidden in a mess of net and branches. He was sobbing with the
effort. He was a big man, and unused to exercise, and sodden
with brandy. He had only one idea in his mind – to stop the guns
firing, to stop them at all costs.

Luckily, there seemed to be a hitch. The lights were still out.
The unearthly graveyard at the end of the square glittered white
in the moonlight. Then the lights briefly switched on, and the
village sprang into existence for just long enough to show large
red crosses all over a white building beside the church. Then
moonlight flooded everything again, and the crosses vanished.
'Oh, the bloody fool!' sobbed the Captain, running, running as if
for his life. He was cutting across a corner of the square direct to
the church. He could hear some officers cursing behind him:
'Who put those red crosses there? Who? We can't fire on the Red
Cross.'

The Captain reached the church as the searchlights burst on.
Inside, Michele was kneeling on the earth looking at his first
Madonna. 'They are going to kill my Madonna,' he said
miserably.

'Come away, Michele, come away.'

'They're going to . . .'

The Captain grabbed his arm and pulled. Michele wrenched
himself free and grabbed a saw. He began hacking at the ceiling
board. There was a dead silence outside. They heard a voice
booming through the loudspeakers: 'The village that is about to
be shelled is an English village, not as represented on the

programme, a German village. Repeat, the village that is about to be shelled is . . .'

Michele had cut through two sides of a square around the Madonna.

'Michele,' sobbed the Captain, '*get out of here.*'

Michele dropped the saw, took hold of the raw edges of the board and tugged. As he did so, the church began to quiver and lean. An irregular patch of board ripped out and Michele staggered back into the Captain's arms. There was a roar. The church seemed to dissolve around them into flame. Then they were running away from it, the Captain holding Michele tight by the arm. 'Get down,' he shouted suddenly, and threw Michele to the earth. He flung himself down beside him. Looking from under the crook of his arm, he heard the explosion, saw a great pillar of smoke and flame, and the village disintegrated in a flying mass of debris. Michele was on his knees gazing at his Madonna in the light from the flame. She was unrecognizable, blotted out with dust. He looked horrible, quite white, and a trickle of blood soaked from his hair down one cheek.

'They shelled my Madonna,' he said.

'Oh, damn it, you can paint another one,' said the Captain. His own voice seemed to him strange, like a dream voice. He was certainly crazy, as mad as Michele himself . . . He got up, pulled Michele to his feet, and marched him towards the edge of the field. There they were met by the ambulance people. Michele was taken off to hospital, and the Captain was sent back to bed.

A week passed. The Captain was in a darkened room. That he was having some kind of a breakdown was clear, and two nurses stood guard over him. Sometimes he lay quiet. Sometimes he muttered to himself. Sometimes he sang in a thick clumsy voice bits out of opera, fragments from Italian songs, and – over and over again – There's a Long Long Trail. He was not thinking of anything at all. He shied away from the thought of Michele as if it were dangerous. When, therefore, a cheerful female voice announced that a friend had come to cheer him up, and it would do him good to have some company, and he saw a white bandage moving towards him in the gloom, he turned sharp over on to his side, face to the wall.

'Go away,' he said. 'Go away, Michele.'

'I have come to see you,' said Michele. 'I have brought you a present.'

The Captain slowly turned over. There was Michele, a cheerful ghost in the dark room. 'You fool,' he said. 'You messed everything up. What did you paint those crosses for?'

'It was a hospital,' said Michele. 'In a village there is a hospital, and on the hospital the Red Cross, the beautiful Red Cross – no?'

'I was nearly court-martialled.'

'It was my fault,' said Michele. 'I was drunk.'

'I was responsible.'

'How could you be responsible when I did it? But it is all over. Are you better?'

'Well, I suppose those crosses saved your life.'

'I did not think,' said Michele. 'I was remembering the kindness of the Red Cross people when we were prisoners.'

'Oh shut up, shut up, shut up.'

'I have brought you a present.'

The Captain peered through the dark. Michele was holding up a picture. It was of a native woman with a baby on her back smiling sideways out of the frame.

Michele said: 'You did not like the haloes. So this time, no haloes. For the Captain – no Madonna.' He laughed. 'You like it? It is for you. I painted it for you.'

'God damn you!' said the Captain.

'You do not like it?' said Michele, very hurt.

The Captain closed his eyes. 'What are you going to do next?' he asked tiredly.

Michele laughed again. 'Mrs Pannerhurst, the lady of the General, she wants me to paint her picture in her white dress. So I paint it.'

'You should be proud to.'

'Silly bitch. She thinks I am good. They know nothing – savages. Barbarians. Not you, Captain, you are my friend. But these people they know nothing.'

The Captain lay quiet. Fury was gathering in him. He thought of the General's wife. He disliked her, but he had known her well enough.

'These people,' said Michele. 'They do not know a good

picture from a bad picture. I paint, I paint, this way, that way. There is the picture – I look at it and laugh inside myself.' Michele laughed out loud. 'They say, he is a Michelangelo, this one, and try to cheat me out of my price. Michele – Michelangelo – that is a joke, no?'

The Captain said nothing.

'But for you I painted this picture to remind you of our good times with the village. You are my friend. I will always remember you.'

The Captain turned his eyes sideways in his head and stared at the black girl. Her smile at him was half innocence, half malice.

'Get out,' he said suddenly.

Michele came closer and bent to see the Captain's face. 'You wish me to go?' He sounded unhappy. 'You saved my life. I was a fool that night. But I was thinking of my offering to the Madonna – I was a fool, I say it myself. I was drunk, we are fools when we are drunk.'

'Get out of here,' said the Captain again.

For a moment the white bandage remained motionless. Then it swept downwards in a bow.

Michele turned towards the door.

'And take that bloody picture with you.'

Silence. Then, in the dim light, the Captain saw Michele reach out for the picture, his white head bowed in profound obeisance. He straightened himself and stood to attention, holding the picture with one hand, and keeping the other stiff down his side. Then he saluted the Captain.

'Yes, *sir*,' he said, and he turned and went out of the door with the picture.

The Captain lay still. He felt – what did he feel? There was a pain under his ribs. It hurt to breathe. He realized he was unhappy. Yes, a terrible unhappiness was filling him, slowly, slowly. He was unhappy because Michele had gone. Nothing had ever hurt the Captain in all his life as much as that mocking *Yes, sir*. Nothing. He turned his face to the wall and wept. But silently. Not a sound escaped him, for the fear the nurses might hear.

The Trinket Box

Yes, but it was only recently, when it became clear that Aunt Maud really could not last much longer, that people began to ask all those questions which should have been asked, it seems now, so long ago.

Or perhaps it is the other way about: Aunt Maud, suddenly finding that innumerable nieces and nephews and cousins were beginning to take an interest in her, asking her to meet interesting people, was so disturbed to find herself pushed into the centre of the stage where she felt herself to be out of place, that she took to her bed where she could tactfully die?

Even here, lying on massed pillows, like a small twig that has been washed up against banks of smooth white sand, she is not left in peace. Distant relations who have done no more than send her Christmas cards once a year come in to see her, sit by her bed for hours at a time, send her flowers. But why? It is not merely that they want to know what London in the 'nineties was like for a young woman with plenty of money, although they wake her to ask: 'Do tell us, do you remember the Oscar Wilde affair?' Her face puckers in a worried look, and she says: 'Oscar Wilde? What? Oh yes, I read such an interesting book, it is in the library.'

Perhaps Aund Maud herself sees that pretty vivacious girl (there is a photograph of her in an album somewhere) as a character in a historical play. But what is that question which it seems everyone comes to ask, but does not ask, leaving at length rather subdued, even a little exasperated – perhaps because it is not like Aunt Maud to suggest unanswerable questions?

Where did it all begin? Some relation returned from a long holiday, and asking casually after the family said: 'What! Aunt

Maud still alive? Isn't she gone yet?' Is that how people began asking: 'Well, but how old is she? Eighty? Ninety?'

'Nonsense, she can't be ninety.'

'But she says she remembers . . .' And the names of old 'incidents' crop up, the sort of thing one finds in dusty books of memoirs. They were another world. It seems impossible that living people can remember them, especially someone we know so well.

'She remembers earlier than that. She told me once – it must be twenty years ago now – of having left home before the Boer War started. You can work that out for yourself.'

'Even that only makes her seventy – eighty perhaps. Eighty is not old enough to get excited about.'

'The Crimean War . . .' But now they laugh. 'Come, come, she's not a hundred!'

No, she cannot be as much as that, but thirty years ago, no less, an old frail lady climbed stiffly but jauntily up the bank of a dried-up African river, where she was looking after a crowd of other people's children on a picnic, and remarked: 'My old bones are getting creaky.' Then she bought herself an ancient car. It was one of the first Ford models, and she went rattling in it over the bad corrugated roads and even over the veld, if there were no roads. And no one thought it extraordinary. Just as one did not think of her as an old maid, or a spinster, so one did not think of her as an old lady.

And then there was the way she used to move from continent to continent, from family to family, as a kind of unpaid servant. For she had no money at all by then: her brother the black sheep died and she insisted on giving up all her tiny capital to pay his debts. It was useless of course; he owed thousands, but no one could persuade her against it. 'There are some things one has to do,' she said. Now, lying in bed she says: 'One doesn't want to be a nuisance,' in her small faded voice; the same voice in which she used to announce, and not so very long ago: 'I am going to South America as companion to Mrs Fripp – she is so very very kind.' For six months, then, she was prepared to wait hand and foot on an old lady years younger than herself simply for the sake of seeing South America? No, we can no longer believe it. We are forced to know that the thought of her aches and pains put

warmth into Mrs Fripp's voice when she asked Aunt Maud to go
with her.

And from the Andes or the Christmas Islands, or some place
as distant and preposterous as the Russian-Japanese war or the
Morocco scramble seem to be in time, came those long long
letters beginning: 'That white dressing-jacket you gave me was
so useful when I went to the mountains.' She got so many
presents from us all that now we feel foolish. They were not what
she wanted, after all.

Then, before we expected it, someone would write and say:
'By the way, did you know I have had Aunt Maud with me since
Easter?' So she had come back from the Andes, or wherever it
was? But why had she gone *there*? Was Anne having another baby
perhaps?

Sitting up in bed surrounded by the cushions and photographs
that framed her in the way other people's furniture frame them,
always very early in the morning – she wrote letters from five to
seven every day of her life – she answered in her tiny precise
handwriting: 'Jacko's leg is not quite healed yet, although I think
he is well on the way to recovery. And then I shall be delighted
to avail myself of your kind offer. I will be with you by the
middle of . . .' Punctually to the hour she would arrive; the
perfect guest. And when she left, because of the arrival of a baby
or a sudden illness perhaps five hundred miles away or in another
country, with what affectionate heart-warming gratitude she
thanked us, until it was easy to forget the piles of mending, the
delicious cooking, the nights and nights of nursing. A week after
she had left would arrive the inevitable parcel, containing
presents so apt that it was with an uneasy feeling that we sat
down to write thanks. How did she come to know our most secret
wants? And, imperceptibly, the unease would grow to resentment. She had no right, no right at all, to give such expensive
presents when she was dependent on relations for her support.

So it was that after every visit a residue of spite and irritation
remained. And perhaps she intended that the people she served
should never have to feel the embarrassment of gratitude?
Perhaps she intended us – who knows? – to think as we sat
writing our thank-yous: But after all, she has to live on us, it is
after all a kindness to feed and house her for a few weeks.

It is all intolerable, intolerable, and it seems now that we must march into that bedroom to ask: 'Aunt Maud, how did you bear it? How could you stand, year in and year out, pouring out your treasures of affection to people who hardly noticed you? Do you realize, Aunt Maud, that now, thirty years or more after you became our servant, it is the first time that we are really aware you were ever alive? What do you, say to that, Aunt Maud? *Or did you know it all the time* . . .' For that is what we want to be sure of: that she did not know it, that she never will.

We wander restlessly in and out of her room, watching that expression on her face which – now that she is too ill to hide what she feels – makes us so uneasy. She looks impatient when she sees us; she wishes we would go away. Yesterday she said: 'One does not care for this kind of attention.'

All the time, all over the house, people sit about talking, talking, in low urgent anxious voices, as if something vital and precious is leaking away as they wait.

'She *can't* be exactly the same, it is impossible!'

'But I tell you, I remember her on the day the war started – the old war, you know. On the platform, waving good-bye to my son. She was the same, wrinkle for wrinkle. That little patch of yellow on her cheek – like an egg-stain. And those little mauvish eyes, and that funny little voice. People don't talk like that now, each syllable sounding separately.'

'Her eyes have changed though.' We sneak in to have a look at her. She turns them on us, peering over the puffs of a pink bedjacket – eyes where a white film is gathering. Unable to see us clearly, afraid – she who has sat by so many death-beds – of distressing us by her unsightliness, she turns away her head, lies back, folds her hands, is silent.

When other people die, it is a thing of horror, swellings, gross flesh, smells, sickness. But Aunt Maud dies as a leaf shrivels. It seems that a little dryish gasp, a little shiver, and the papery flesh will crumble and leave beneath the bedclothes she scarcely disturbs a tiny white skeleton. That is how she is dying, giving the least possible trouble to the niece who waited sharp-sightedly for someone else to use the phrase 'a happy release' before she used it herself. 'She might not eat anything, but one has to prepare the tray all the same. And then, there are all these people in the house.'

'Before she retired, what did she do?'

'Taught, didn't you know? She was forty when her father married again, and she went out and took a post in a school. He never spoke one word to her afterwards.'

'But why, why?'

'He was in the wrong of course. She didn't marry so as to look after him.'

'Oh, so she might have married? Who was he?'

'Old John Jordan, do you remember?'

'But he died before I left school – such a funny old man!'

Impossible to ask why she never married. But someone asks it. A great-niece, very young, stands beside the bed and looks down with shivering distaste at such age, such death: 'Aunt Maud, why did you never marry?'

'Marry! Marry! Who is talking about marrying?' she sounds angered and sullen; then the small eyes film over and she says: 'Who did you say is getting married?'

The niece is banished and there are no more questions.

No more visitors either, the doctor says. A question of hours. A few hours, and that casket of memories and sensations will have vanished. It is monstrous that a human being who has survived miraculously and precariously so many decades of war, illnesses and accidents should die at last, leaving behind nothing.

Now we sit about the bed where she lies and wait for her to die. There is nothing to do. No one stirs. We are all sitting, looking, thinking, surreptitiously touching the things that belonged to her, trying to catch a glimpse, even for a moment, of the truth that will vanish in such a little while.

And if we think of the things that interested her, the enthusiasms we used to laugh at, because it seemed so odd that such an old lady should feel strongly about these great matters, what answer do we get? She was a feminist, first and foremost. The Pankhursts, she said, 'were so devoted'. She was a socialist; she had letters from Keir Hardie. There had been no one like him since he died. She defended vegetarians, but would not be one herself, because it gave people so much trouble in the kitchen. Madame Curie, Charles Lindbergh, Marie Corelli, Lenin, Clara

Butt – these were here Idols, and she spoke of them in agitated defiance as if they were always in need of defence. Inside that tiny shrivelled skull what an extraordinary gallery of heroes and heroines. But there was no answer there. No matter how hard we try, fingering her handkerchief sachet, thinking of the funny flat hats she wore, draped with bits of Liberty cottons, remembering how she walked, as if at any moment she might be called upon to scale a high wall, she eludes us. Let us resign ourselves to it and allow her to die.

Then she speaks, after such long hours of waiting it is as if a woman already dead were speaking. Now, now! We lean forward, waiting for her to say just that one thing, the perfect word of forgiveness that will leave us healed and whole.

She has made her will, she says, and it is with the lawyer 'who has always been so kind to her'. She has nothing to leave but a few personal trinkets . . . The small precise voice breathless, and she keeps her eyes tight shut. 'I have told my lawyer that my possessions, such as they are, are kept in my black trinket box in the cupboard there. He knows. Everything is in order. I put everything right when people became so kind and I knew I was ill.'

And that is the last thing she will ever say. We wait intently, shifting our feet and avoiding each other's eyes for fear that our guilty glances may imprint upon our memories of her the terrible knowledge let slip in the order of the words of that final sentence. We do not want to remember her with guilt, oh no! But although we wait, straining, nothing else comes; she seems to be asleep, and slowly we let our limbs loosen and think of the black box. In it we will find the diaries, or the bundle of letters which will say what she refuses to say. Oh most certainly we will find something of that sort. She cannot die like this, leaving nothing. There will be evidence of a consumed sorrow, at the least, something that will put substance into this barrenness. And when at last we look up, glancing at our watches, we see there is a stillness in the tiny white face which means she is dead.

We get up, rather stiffly, because of the hours of sitting, and then after a decent interval open the black box. It is full to the brim with bits of lace and ribbon, scraps of flowery stuffs, buckles, braid, brooches, cheap glass necklaces. Each has a bit of paper pinned to it. 'These buttons I thought would do for the frock Alice was making when I was there last month.' And: 'To little Robin with my fond love. I bought this glass peacock in Cape Town in 1914 for another little boy.' And so on, each of us has something. And when we come to the end and search for the diaries and letters there is nothing! Secretively each of us taps at the wood of the bottom – but no, it is solid. And we put back the things and we feel for the first time that Aunt Maud is dead. We want to cry. We would, if it were not absurd to cry for an old woman whom none of us wanted. What would she say if she saw those tears? 'One cannot help feeling it would have been more useful to feel for me when I was still alive'? No, she would never say a thing like that; but we can have no illusions now, after that last remark of hers, which revealed the Aunt Maud she had been so carefully concealing all these years. And she would know we were not weeping for her at all.

We cannot leave the black box. We finger the laces, stroke the wood. We come back to it again and again, where it lies on the table in the room in which she is waiting for the funeral people. We do not look at her, who is now no more than a tiny bundle under the clothes. And slowly, slowly, in each of us, an emotion hardens which is painful because it can never be released. Protest, is that what we are feeling? But certainly a protest without bitterness, for she was never bitter. And without pity, for one cannot imagine Aunt Maud pitying herself. What, then, is left? Are we expected to go on, for the rest of our lives (which we hope will be as long as hers) feeling this intolerable ache, a dull and sorrowful rage? And if we all feel, suddenly, that it is not to be borne, and we must leap up from our chairs and bang our fists against the wall screaming: 'No, no! It can't all be for nothing!' – then we must restrain ourselves and remain quietly seated; for we can positively hear the scrupulous little voice saying: 'There are some things one does not do.'

Slowly, slowly, we become still before the box, and now it seems that we hold Aunt Maud in the hollow of our palms. That was what she was; now we know her.

So it comes to this: we are grown proud and honest out of the knowledge of her honesty and pride and, measuring ourselves against her we allow ourselves to feel only the small, persistent, but gently humorous anger she must have felt. Only anger, that is permissible, she would allow that. But against what? Against what?

The Pig

The farmer paid his labourers on a Saturday evening, when the sun went down. By the time he had finished it was always quite dark, and from the kitchen door where the lantern hung, bars of yellow light lay down the steps, across the path, and lit up the trees and the dark faces under them.

This Saturday, instead of dispersing as usual when they took their money, they retired a little way into the dark under the foliage, talking among themselves to pass the time. When the last one had been paid, the farmer said: 'Call the women and the children. Everybody in the compound must be here.' The boss-boy, who had been standing beside the table calling out names, stood forward and repeated the order. But in an indifferent voice, as a matter of form, for all this had happened before, every year for years past. Already there was a subdued moving at the back of the crowd as the women came in from under the trees where they had been waiting; and the light caught a bunched skirt, a copper armlet, or a bright headcloth.

Now all the dimly-lit faces showed hope that soon this ritual would be over, and they could get back to their huts and their fires. They crowded closer without being ordered.

The farmer began to speak, thinking as he did so of his lands that lay all about him, invisible in the darkness, but sending on the wind a faint rushing noise like the sea; and although he had done this before so often, and was doing it now half-cynically, knowing it was a waste of time, the memory of how good those fields of strong young plants looked when the sun shone on them put urgency and even anger into his voice.

The trouble was that every year black hands stripped the cobs from the stems in the night, sacks of cobs; and he could never catch the thieves. Next morning he would see the prints of bare feet in the dust between the rows. He had tried everything; had warned, threatened, docked rations, even fined the whole compound collectively – it made no difference. The lands lying next to the compounds would be cheated of their yield, and when the harvesters brought in their loads, everyone knew there would be less than what had been expected.

And if everyone knew it, why put on this display for the tenth time? That was the question the farmer saw on the faces in front of him; polite faces turning this way and that over impatient bodies and shifting feet. They were thinking only of the huts and the warm meal waiting for them. The philosophic politeness, almost condescension, with which he was being treated infuriated the farmer; and he stopped in the middle of a sentence, banging on the table with his fist, so that the faces centred on him and the feet stilled.

'Jonas,' said the farmer. Out on to the lit space stepped a tall elderly man with a mild face. But now he looked sombre. The farmer saw that look and braced himself for a fight. This man had been on the farm for several years. An old scoundrel, the farmer called him, but affectionately: he was fond of him, for they had been together for so long. Jonas did odd jobs for half the year; he drew water for the garden, cured hides, cut grass. But when the growing season came he was an important man.

'Come here, Jonas,' the farmer said again; and picked up the .33 rifle that had been leaning against his chair until now. During the rainy season, Jonas slept out his days in his hut, and spent his nights till the cold dawns came guarding the fields from the buck and the pigs that attacked the young plants. They could lay waste whole acres in one night, a herd of pigs. He took the rifle, greeting it, feeling its familiar weight on his arm. But he looked reluctant nevertheless.

'This year, Jonas, you will shoot everything you see – understand?'

'Yes, baas.'

'Everything, buck, baboons, pig. And everything you hear. You will not stop to look. If you hear a noise, you will shoot.'

There was a movement among the listening people, and soft protesting noises.

'And if it turns out to be a human pig, then so much the worse. My lands are no place for pigs of any kind.'

Jonas said nothing, but he turned towards the others, holding the rifle uncomfortably on his arm, appealing that they should not judge him.

'You can go,' said the farmer. After a moment the space in front of him was empty, and he could hear the sound of bare feet feeling their way along dark paths, the sound of loudening angry talk. Jonas remained beside him.

'Well, Jonas?'

'I do not want to shoot this year.'

The farmer waited for an explanation. He was not disturbed at the order he had given. In all the years he had worked this farm no one had been shot, although every season the thieves moved at night along the mealie rows, and every night Jonas was out with a gun. For he would shout, or fire the gun into the air, to frighten intruders. It was only when dawn came that he fired at something he could see. All this was a bluff. The threat might scare off a few of the more timid; but both sides knew, as usual, that it was a bluff. The cobs would disappear; nothing could prevent it.

'And why not?' asked the farmer at last.

'It's my wife. I wanted to see you about it before,' said Jonas, in dialect.

'Oh, your wife!' The farmer had remembered. Jonas was old-fashioned. He had two wives, an old one who had borne him several children, and a young one who gave him a good deal of trouble. Last year, when his wife was new, he had not wanted to take on this job which meant being out all night.

'And what is the matter with the day-time?' asked the farmer with waggish good-humour, exactly as he had the year before. He got up, and prepared to go inside.

Jonas did not reply. He did not like being appointed official guardian against theft by his own people, but even that did not matter so much, for it never once occurred to him to take the order literally. This was only the last straw. He was getting on in years now, and he wanted to spend his nights in peace in his own hut, instead of roaming the bush. He had disliked it very much last year but now it was even worse. A younger man visited his pretty young wife when he was away.

Once he had snatched up a stick, in despair, to beat her with; then he had thrown it down. He was old, and the other man was young, and beating her could not cure his heartache. Once he had come up to his master to talk over the situation, as man to man; but the farmer had refused to do anything. And, indeed, what could he do? Now, repeating what he had said then, the farmer spoke from the kitchen steps, holding the lamp high in one hand above his shoulder as he turned to go in, so that it sent beams of light swinging across the bush: 'I don't want to hear anything about your wife, Jonas. You should look after her yourself. And if you are not too old to take a young wife, then you aren't too old to shoot. You will take the gun as usual this year. Good night.' And he went inside, leaving the garden black and pathless. Jonas stood quite still, waiting for his eyes to accustom themselves to the dark; then he started off down the path, finding his way by the feel of the loose stones under his feet.

He had not yet eaten, but when he came to within sight of the compound, he felt he could not go farther. He halted, looking at the little huts silhouetted black against cooking fires that sent up great drifting clouds of illuminated smoke. There was his hut, he could see it, a small conical shape. There his wives were, waiting with his food prepared and ready.

But he did not want to eat. He felt he could not bear to go in and face his old wife, who mocked him with her tongue, and his young wife who answered him submissively but mocked him with her actions. He was sick and tormented, cut off from his friends who were preparing for an evening by the fires, because he could see the knowledge of his betrayal in their eyes. The cold pain of jealousy that had been gnawing at him for so long, felt now like an old wound, aching as an old wound aches before the rains set in.

He did not want to go into the fields, either to perch until he was stiff in one of the little cabins on high stilts that were built at the corners of each land as shooting platforms, or to walk in the dark through the hostile bush. But that night, without going for his food, he set off as usual on his long vigil.

The next night, however, he did not go; nor the next, nor the nights following. He lay all day dozing in the sun on his blanket, turning himself over and over in the sun, as if its rays could cauterize the ache from his heart. When evening came, he ate his meal early before going off with the gun. And then he stood with his back to a tree, within sight of the compound; indeed, within a stone's throw of his own hut, for hours, watching silently. He felt numb and heavy. He was there without purpose. It was as if his legs had refused an order to march away from the place. All that week the lands lay unguarded, and if the wild animals were raiding the young plants, he did not care. He seemed to exist only in order to stand at night watching his hut. He did not allow himself to think of what was happening inside. He merely watched; until the fires burned down, and the bush grew cold and he was so stiff that when he went home, at sunrise, he had the appearance of one exhausted after a night's walking.

The following Saturday there was a beer drink. He could have got leave to attend it, had he wanted; but at sundown he took himself off as usual and saw that his wife was pleased when he left.

As he leaned his back to the tree trunk that gave him its support each night, and held the rifle lengthwise to his chest, he fixed his eyes steadily on the dark shape that was his hut, and remembered that look on his young wife's face. He allowed himself to think steadily of it, and of many similar things. He remembered the young man, as he had seen him only a few days before, bending over the girl as she knelt to grind meal, laughing with her; then the way they both looked up, startled, at his approach, their faces growing blank.

He could feel his muscles tautening against the rifle as he pictured that scene, so that he set it down on the ground, for relief, letting his arms fall. But in spite of the pain, he continued to think, for tonight things were changed in him, and he no longer felt numb and purposeless. He stood erect and vigilant, letting the long cold barrel slide between his fingers, the hardness of the tree at his back like a second spine. And as he thought of the young man another picture crept into his mind again and again, that of a young water-buck he had shot last year, lying soft at his feet, its tongue slipping out into the dust as he picked

it up, so newly dead that he imagined he felt the blood still
pulsing under the warm skin. And from the small wet place
under its neck a few sticky drops rolled over glistening fur.
Suddenly, as he stood there thinking of the blood, and the limp
dead body of the buck, and the young man laughing with his
wife, his mind grew clear and cool and the oppression on him
lifted.

He sighed deeply, and picked up the rifle again, holding it
close, like a friend, against him, while he gazed in through the
trees at the compound.

It was early, and the flush from sunset had not yet quite gone
from the sky, although where he stood among the undergrowth it
was night. In the clear spaces between the huts groups of figures
took shape, talking and laughing and getting ready for the dance.
Small cooking fires were being lit; and a big central fire blazed,
sending up showers of sparks into the clouds of smoke. The tom-
toms were beating softly; soon the dance would begin. Visitors
were coming in through the bush from other farm compounds
miles away: it would be a long wait.

Three times he heard soft steps along the path close to him
before he drew back and turned his head to watch the young
man pass, as he had passed every night that week, with a jaunty
eager tread and eyes directed towards Jonas' hut. Jonas stood as
quiet as a tree struck by lightning, holding his breath, although
he could not be seen, because the thick shadows from the trees
were black around him. He watched the young man thread his
way through the huts into the circle of firelight, and pass
cautiously to one side of the groups of waiting people, like
someone uncertain of his welcome, before going in through the
door of his own hut.

Hours passed, and he watched the leaping dancing people,
and listened to the drums as the stars swung over his head and
the night birds talked in the bush around him. He thought
steadily now, as he had not previously allowed himself to think,
of what was happening inside the small dark hut that gradually
became invisible as the fires died and the dancers went to their
blankets. When the moon was small and high and cold behind
his back, and the trees threw sharp black shadows on the path,
and he could smell morning on the wind, he saw the young man

coming towards him again. Now Jonas shifted his feet a little, to ease the stiffness out of them, and moved the rifle along his arm, feeling for the curve of the trigger on his finger.

As the young man lurched past, for he was tired, and moved carelessly, Jonas slipped out into the smooth dusty path a few paces behind, shrinking back as the released branches swung wet into his face and scattered large drops of dew on to his legs. It was cold; his breath misted into a thin pearly steam dissolving into the moonlight.

He was so close to the man in front that he could have touched him with the raised rifle; had he turned there would have been no concealment; but Jonas walked confidently, though carefully, and thought all the time of how he had shot down from ten paces away that swift young buck as it started with a crash out of a bush into a cold moony field.

When they reached the edge of the land where acres of mealies sloped away, dimly green under the dome of stars, Jonas began to walk like a cat. He wanted now to be sure; and he was only fifty yards from the shooting platform in the corner of the field, that looked in this light like a crazy fowl-house on stilts. The young man was staggering with tiredness and drink, making a crashing noise at each step as he snapped the sap-full mealies under heavy feet.

But the buck had shot like a spear from the bush, had caught the lead in its chest as it leaped, had fallen as a spear curves to earth; it had not blundered and lurched and swayed. Jonas began to feel a disgust for this man, and the admiration and fascination he felt for his young rival vanished. The tall slim youth who had laughed down at his wife had nothing to do with the ungainly figure crashing along before him, making so much noise that there could be no game left unstartled for miles.

When they reached the shooting platform, Jonas stopped dead, and let the youth move on. He lifted the rifle to his cheek and saw the long barrel slant against the stars, which sent a glint of light back down the steel. He waited, quite still, watching the man's back sway above the mealies. Then, at the right moment, he squeezed his finger close, holding the rifle ready to fire again.

As the sound of the shot reverberated, the round black head jerked oddly, blotting out fields of stars; the body seemed to crouch, and one hand went out as if he were going to lean sideways to the ground. Then he disappeared into the mealies with a startled thick cry. Jonas lowered the rifle and listened. There was a threshing noise, a horrible grunting, and half-words muttered, like someone talking in sleep.

Jonas picked his way along the rows, feeling the sharp leaf edges scything his legs, until he stood above the body that now jerked softly among the stems. He waited until it stilled, then bent to look, parting the chilled, moon-green leaves so that he could see clearly.

It was no clean small hole: raw flesh gaped, blood poured black to the earth, the limbs were huddled together shapeless and without beauty, the face was pressed into the soil.

'A pig,' said Jonas aloud to the listening moon, as he kicked the side gently with his foot, 'nothing but a pig.'

He wanted to hear how it would sound when he said it again, telling how he had shot blind into the grunting, invisible herd.

Traitors

We had discovered the Thompsons' old house long before their first visit.

At the back of our house the ground sloped up to where the bush began, an acre of trailing pumpkin vines, ash-heaps where pawpaw trees sprouted, and lines draped with washing where the wind slapped and jiggled. The bush was dense and frightening, and the grass there higher than a tall man. There were not even paths.

When we had tired of our familiar acre we explored the rest of the farm: but this particular stretch of bush was avoided. Sometimes we stood at its edge, and peered in at the tangled granite outcrops and great ant-heaps curtained with Christmas fern. Sometimes we pushed our way in a few feet, till the grass closed behind us, leaving overhead a small space of blue. Then we lost our heads and ran back again.

Later, when we were given our first rifle and a new sense of bravery, we realized we had to challenge that bush. For several days we hesitated, listening to the guinea-fowl calling only a hundred yards away, and making excuses for cowardice. Then, one morning, at sunrise, when the trees were pink and gold, and the grass-stems were running bright drops of dew, we looked at each other, smiling weakly, and slipped into the bushes with our hearts beating.

At once we were alone, closed in by grass, and we had to reach out for the other's dress and cling together. Slowly, heads down, eyes half closed against the sharp grass-seeds, two small girls pushed their way past ant-heap and outcrop, past thorn and gully and thick clumps of cactus where any wild animal might lurk.

Suddenly, after only five minutes of terror, we emerged in a space where the red earth was scored with cattle tracks. The guinea-fowl were clinking ahead of us in the grass, and we caught a glimpse of a shapely dark bird speeding along a path. We followed, shouting with joy because the forbidding patch of bush was as easily conquered and made our own as the rest of the farm.

We were stopped again when the ground dropped suddenly to the vlei, a twenty-foot shelf of flattened grass where the cattle went to water. Sitting, we lifted our dresses and coasted downhill on the slippery swathes, landing with torn knickers and scratched knees in a donga of red dust scattered with dried cow-pats and bits of glistening quartz. The guinea-fowl stood in a file and watched us, their heads tilted with apprehension; but my sister said, with bravado: 'I am going to shoot a buck!'

She waved her arms at the birds and they scuttled off. We looked at each other and laughed, feeling too grown-up for guinea-fowl now.

Here, down on the verges of the vlei, it was a different kind of bush. The grass was thinned by cattle, and red dust spurted as we walked. There were sparse thorn trees, and everywhere the poison-apple bush, covered with small fruit like yellow plums. Patches of wild marigold filled the air with a rank, hot smell.

Moving with exaggerated care, our bodies tensed, our eyes fixed half a mile off, we did not notice that a duiker stood watching us ten paces away. We yelled with excitement and the buck vanished. Then we ran like maniacs, screaming at the tops of our voices, while the bushes whipped our faces and the thorns tore our legs.

Ten minutes later we came slap up against a barbed fence. 'The boundary,' we whispered, awed. This was a legend; we had imagined it as a sort of Wall of China, for beyond were thousands and thousands of miles of unused Government land where there were leopards and baboons and herds of koodoo. But we were disappointed: even the famous boundary was only a bit of wire after all, and the duiker was nowhere in sight.

Whistling casually to show we didn't care, we marched along by the wire, twanging it so that it reverberated half a mile away down in the vlei. Around us the bush was strange; this part of the farm was quite new to us. There was still nothing but thorn trees and grass; and fat wood-pigeons cooed from every branch. We swung on the fence stanchions and wished that Father would suddenly appear and take us home for breakfast. We were hopelessly lost.

It was then that I saw the pawpaw tree. I must have been staring at it for some minutes before it grew in on my sight; for it was such an odd place for a pawpaw tree to be. On it were three heavy yellow pawpaws.

'There's our breakfast,' I said.

We shook them down, sat on the ground, and ate. The insipid, creamy flesh soon filled us, and we lay down, staring at the sky, half asleep. The sun blared down; we were melted through with heat and tiredness. But it was very hard. Turning over, staring, we saw worn bricks set into the ground. All round us were stretches of brick, stretches of cement.

'The old Thompson house,' we whispered.

And all at once the pigeons seemed to grow still and the bush became hostile. We sat up, frightened. How was it we hadn't noticed it before? There was a double file of pawpaws among the thorns; a purple bougainvillaea tumbled over the bushes; a rose tree scattered white petals at our feet; and our shoes were scrunching in broken glass.

It was desolate, lonely, despairing, and we remembered the way our parents had talked about Mr Thompson who had lived here for years before he married. Their hushed, disapproving voices seemed to echo out of the trees; and in a violent panic we picked up the gun and fled back in the direction of the house. We had imagined we were lost; but we were back in the gully in no time, climbed up it, half sobbing with breathlessness, and fled through the barrier of bush so fast we hardly noticed it was there.

It was not even breakfast-time.

'We found the Thompsons' old house,' we said at last, feeling hurt that no one had noticed from our proud faces that we had found a whole new world that morning.

'Did you?' said Father absently. 'Can't be much left of it now.'

Our fear vanished. We hardly dared look at each other for shame. And after that day we went back and counted the pawpaws and trailed the bougainvillaea over a tree and staked the white rosebush.

In a week we had made the place entirely our own. We were there all day, sweeping the debris from the floor and carrying away loose bricks into the bush. We were not surprised to find dozens of empty bottles scattered in the grass. We washed them in a pothole in the vlei, dried them in the wind, and marked out the rooms of the house with them, making walls of shining bottles. In our imagination the Thompson house was built again, a small brick-walled place with a thatched roof.

We sat under a blazing sun, and said in our Mother's voice: 'It is always cool under thatch, no matter how hot it is outside.' And then, when the walls and the roof had grown into our minds and we took them for granted, we played other games, taking it in turn to be Mr Thompson.

Whoever was Mr Thompson had to stagger in from the bush, with a bottle in her hand, tripping over the lintel and falling on the floor. There she lay and groaned, while the other fanned her and put handkerchiefs soaked in vlei water on her head. Or she reeled about among the bottles, shouting abusive gibberish at an invisible audience of natives. We were not brought up in a farming district for nothing.

It was while we were engaged thus, one day, that a native woman came out of the thorn trees and stood watching us. We waited for her to go, drawing together; but she came close and stared in a way that made us afraid. She was old and fat, and she wore a red print dress from the store. She said in a soft, wheedling voice: 'When is Boss Thompson coming back?'

'Go away!' we shouted. And then she began to laugh. She sauntered off into the bush, swinging her hips and looking back over her shoulder and laughing. We heard that taunting laugh away among the trees; and that was the second time we ran away from the ruined house, though we made ourselves walk slowly and with dignity until we knew she could no longer see us.

For a few days we didn't go back to the house. When we did we stopped playing Mr Thompson. We no longer knew him; that laugh, that slow, insulting stare had meant something outside our knowledge and experience. The house was not ours now. It was some broken bricks on the ground marked out with bottles.

We couldn't pretend to ourselves we were not afraid of the place; and we continually glanced over our shoulders to see if the old native woman was standing silently there, watching us.

Idling along the fence, we threw stones at the pawpaws fifteen feet over our heads till they squashed at our feet. Then we kicked them into the bush.

'Why have you stopped going to the old house?' asked Mother cautiously, thinking that we didn't know how pleased she was. She had instinctively disliked our being there so much.

'Oh, I dunno . . .'

A few days later we heard that the Thompsons were coming to see us; and we knew, without anyone saying anything, that this was no ordinary visit. It was the first time; they wouldn't be coming after all these years without some reason. Besides, our parents didn't like them coming. They were at odds with each other over it.

Mr Thompson had lived on our farm for ten years before we had it, when there was no one else near for miles and miles. Then, suddenly, he went home to England and brought a wife back with him. The wife never came to this farm. Mr Thompson sold the farm to us and bought another one. People said:

'Poor girl! Just out from home, too.' She was angry about the house burning down, because it meant she had to live with the friends for nearly a year while Mr Thompson built a new house on his new farm.

The night before they came, Mother said several times in a strange, sorrowful voice, 'Poor little thing; poor, poor little thing.'

Father said: 'Oh, I don't know. After all, be just. He was here alone all those years.'

It was no good; she disliked not only Mr Thompson but Father too, that evening; and we were on her side. She put her arms round us, and looked accusingly at Father. 'Women get all the worst of everything,' she said.

When Mother started talking like that, which she did some-times, Father used to light his pipe and go for a walk. But tonight he said angrily: 'Look here, it's not my fault these people are coming.'

'Who said it was?' she answered.

*   *   *

Next day, when the car came in sight, we vanished into the bush. We felt guilty, not because we were running away, a thing we often did when visitors came we didn't like, but because we had made Mr Thompson's house our own, and because we were afraid if he saw our faces he would know we were letting Mother down by going.

We climbed into the tree that was our refuge on these occasions, and lay along branches twenty feet from the ground, and played at Mowgli, thinking all the time about the Thompsons.

As usual, we lost all sense of time; and when we eventually returned, thinking the coast must be clear, the car was still there. Curiosity got the better of us.

We slunk on to the verandah, smiling bashfully, while Mother gave us a reproachful look. Then, at last, we lifted our heads and looked at Mrs Thompson. I don't know how we had imagined her; but we had felt for her a passionate, protective pity.

She was a large, blonde, brilliantly coloured lady with a voice like a go-away bird's. It was a horrible voice. Father, who could not stand loud voices, was holding the arms of his chair, and gazing at her with exasperated dislike. Mother had a polite, vacant smile; and in her voice was a note that meant she was being loyal to something against her personal inclinations. We knew that note well.

As for Mr Thompson, that villain whom we had hated and feared, he was a shaggy and shambling man, who looked at the ground while his wife talked, with a small apologetic smile. He was not in the least as we had pictured him. He looked like our old dog. For a moment we were confused; then, in a rush, our allegiance shifted. The profound and dangerous pity, aroused in us earlier than we could remember by the worlds of loneliness inhabited by our parents, which they could not share with each other but each shared with us, settled now in Mr Thompson. Now we hated Mrs Thompson. The outward sign of it was that we left Mother's chair and went to Father's.

'Don't fidget, there's good kids,' he said.

Mrs Thompson was asking to be shown the old house. We understood, from the insistent sound of her voice, that she had been talking about nothing else all afternoon; or that, at any rate, if she had, it was only with the intention of getting round to the house as soon as she could. She kept saying, smiling ferociously at Mr Thompson: 'I have heard such *interesting* things about that old place. I really must see for myself where it was that my husband lived before I came out . . .' And she looked at Mother for approval.

But Mother said dubiously: 'It will soon be dark. And there is no path.'

As for Father, he said bluntly: 'There's nothing to be seen. There's nothing left.'

'Yes, I heard it had been burnt down,' said Mrs Thompson with another look at her husband.

'It was a hurricane lamp . . .' he muttered.

'I want to see for myself.'

At this point my sister slipped off the arm of my Father's chair, and said, with a bright, false smile at Mrs Thompson, 'We know where it is. We'll take you.' She dug me in the ribs and sped off before anyone could speak.

At last they all decided to come. I took them the hardest, longest way I knew. We had made a path of our own long ago, but that would have been too quick. I made Mrs Thompson climb over rocks, push through grass, bend under bushes. I made her scramble down the gully so that she fell on her knees in the sharp pebbles and the dust. I walked her so fast, finally, in a wide circle through the thorn trees that I could hear her panting behind me. But she wasn't complaining: she wanted to see the place too badly.

When we came to where the house had been it was nearly dark and the tufts of long grass were shivering in the night breeze, and the pawpaw trees were silhouetted high and dark against a red sky. Guinea-fowl were clinking softly all around us.

My sister leaned against a tree, breathing hard, trying to look natural. Mrs Thompson had lost her confidence. She stood quite still, looking about her, and we knew the silence and the desolation had got her, as it got us that first morning.

'But *where* is the house?' she asked at last, unconsciously softening her voice, staring as if she expected to see it rise out of the ground in front of her.

'I told you, it was burnt down. *Now* will you believe me?' said Mr Thompson.

'I *know* it was burnt down . . . Well, where was it then?' She sounded as if she was going to cry. This was not at all what she had expected.

Mr Thompson pointed at the bricks on the ground. He did not move. He stood staring over the fence down to the vlei, where the mist was gathering in long white folds. The light faded out of the sky, and it began to get cold. For a while no one spoke.

'What a god-forsaken place for a house,' said Mrs Thompson, very irritably, at last. 'Just as well it was burnt down. Do you mean to say your kids play here?'

That was our cue. 'We like it,' we said dutifully, knowing very well that the two of us standing on the bricks, hand in hand, beside the ghostly rose bush, made a picture that took all the harm out of the place for her. 'We play here all day,' we lied.

'Odd taste you've got,' she said, speaking at us, but meaning Mr Thompson.

Mr Thompson did not hear her. He was looking around with a lost, remembering expression. 'Ten years,' he said at last. 'Ten years I was here.'

'More fool you,' she snapped. And that closed the subject as far as she was concerned.

We began to trail home. Now the two women went in front; then came Father and Mr Thompson; we followed at the back. As we passed a small donga under a cactus tree, my sister called in a whisper, 'Mr Thompson, Mr Thompson, look here.'

Father and Mr Thompson came back. 'Look,' we said, pointing to the hole that was filled to the brim with empty bottles.

'I came quickly by a way of my own and hid them,' said my sister proudly, looking at the two men like a conspirator.

Father was very uncomfortable. 'I wonder how they got down here?' he said politely at last.

'We found them. They were at the house. We hid them for you,' said my sister, dancing with excitement.

Mr Thompson looked at us sharply and uneasily. 'You are an odd pair of kids,' he said.

That was all the thanks we got from him; for then we heard

Mother calling from ahead: 'What are you all doing there?' And at once we went forward.

After the Thompsons had left we hung around Father, waiting for him to say something.

At last, when Mother wasn't there, he scratched his head in an irritable way and said: 'What in the world did you do that for?'

We were bitterly hurt. '*She* might have seen them,' I said.

'Nothing would make much difference to that lady,' he said at last. 'Still, I suppose you meant well.'

We drifted off; we felt let down.

In the corner of the verandah, in the dark, sat Mother, gazing into the dark bush. On her face was a grim look of disapproval, and distaste and unhappiness. We were included in it, we knew that.

She looked at us crossly and said, 'I don't like you wandering over the farm the way you do. Even with a gun.'

But she had said that so often, and it wasn't what we were waiting for. At last it came.

'My two little girls,' she said, 'out in the bush by themselves, with no one to play with . . .'

It wasn't the bush she minded. We flung ourselves on her. Once again we were swung dizzily from one camp to the other. 'Poor Mother,' we said. 'Poor, poor Mother.'

That was what she needed. 'It's no life for a woman, this,' she said, her voice breaking, gathering us close.

But she sounded comforted.

The Old Chief Mshlanga

They were good, the years of ranging the bush over her father's farm which, like every white farm, was largely unused, broken only occasionally by small patches of cultivation. In between, nothing but trees, the long sparse grass – thorn and cactus and gully, grass and outcrop and thorn. And a jutting piece of rock which had been thrust up from the warm soil of Africa unimaginable eras of time ago, washed into hollows and whorls by sun and wind that had travelled so many thousands of miles of space and bush, would hold the weight of a small girl whose eyes were sightless for anything but a pale willowed river, a pale gleaming castle – a small girl singing: 'Out flew the web and floated wide, the mirror cracked from side to side . . .'

Pushing her way through the green aisles of the mealie stalks, the leaves arching like cathedrals veined with sunlight far overhead, with the packed red earth underfoot, a fine lace of red-starred witchweed would summon up a black bent figure croaking premonitions: the Northern witch, bred of cold Northern forests, would stand before her among the mealie fields, and it was the mealie fields that faded and fled, leaving her among the gnarled roots of an oak, snow falling thick and soft and white, the wood-cutter's fire glowing red welcome through crowding tree trunks.

A white child, opening its eyes curiously on a sun-suffused landscape, a gaunt and violent landscape, might be supposed to accept it as her own, to take the msasa trees and the thorn trees as familiar, to feel her blood running free and responsive to the swing of the seasons.

This child could not see a msasa tree, or the thorn, for what they were. Her books held tales of alien fairies, her rivers ran slow and peaceful, and she knew the shape of the leaves of an ash

or an oak, the names of the little creatues that lived in English
streams, when the words 'the veld' meant strangeness, though
she could remember nothing else.

Because of this, for many years, it was the veld that seemed
unreal; the sun was a foreign sun, and the wind spoke a strange
language.

The black people on the farm were as remote as the trees and
the rocks. They were an amorphous black mass, mingling and
thinning and massing like tadpoles, faceless, who existed merely
to serve, to say 'Yes, Baas,' take their money and go. They
changed season by season, moving from one farm to the next,
according to their outlandish needs, which one did not have to
understand, coming from perhaps hundreds of miles North or
East, passing on after a few months – where? Perhaps even as far
away as the fabled gold mines of Johannesburg, where the pay
was so much better than the few shillings a month and the
double handful of mealie meal twice a day which they earned in
that part of Africa.

The child was taught to take them for granted: the servants in
the house would come running a hundred yards to pick up a
book if she dropped it. She was called 'Nkosikaas' – Chieftainess,
even by the black children her own age.

Later, when the farm grew too small to hold her curiosity, she
carried a gun in the crook of her arm and wandered miles a day,
from vlei to vlei, from kopje to kopje, accompanied by two dogs:
the dogs and the gun were an armour against fear. Because of
them she never felt fear.

If a native came into sight along the kaffir paths half a mile
away, the dogs would flush him up a tree as if he were a bird. If
he expostulated (in his uncouth language which was by itself
ridiculous) that was cheek. If one was in a good mood, it could
be a matter for laughter. Otherwise one passed on, hardly
glancing at the angry native in the tree.

On the rare occasions when white children met together they
could amuse themselves by hailing a passing native in order to
make a buffoon of him; they could set the dogs on him and watch
him run; they could tease a small black child as if he were a
puppy – save that they would not throw stones and sticks at a
dog without a sense of guilt.

Later still, certain questions presented themselves in the child's mind; and because the answers were not easy to accept, they were silenced by an even greater arrogance of manner.

It was even impossible to think of the black people who worked about the house as friends, for if she talked to one of them, her mother would come running anxiously: 'Come away; you mustn't talk to natives.'

It was this instilled consciousness of danger, of something unpleasant, that made it easy to laugh out loud, crudely, if a servant made a mistake in his English or if he failed to understand an order – there is a certain kind of laughter that is fear, afraid of itself.

One evening, when I was about fourteen, I was walking down the side of a mealie field that had been newly ploughed, so that the great red clods showed fresh and tumbling to the vlei beyond, like a choppy red sea; it was that hushed and listening hour, when the birds send long sad calls from tree to tree, and all the colours of earth and sky and leaf are deep and golden. I had my rifle in the curve of my arm, and the dogs were at my heels.

In front of me, perhaps a couple of hundred yards away, a group of three natives came into sight around the side of a big ant-heap. I whistled the dogs close in to my skirts and let the gun swing in my hand, and advanced, waiting for them to move aside, off the path, in respect for my passing. But they came on steadily, and the dogs looked up at me for the command to chase. I was angry. It was 'cheek' for a native not to stand off a path, the moment he caught sight of you.

In front walked an old man, stooping his weight on to a stick, his hair grizzled white, a dark red blanket slung over his shoulders like a cloak. Behind him came two young men, carrying bundles of pots, assegais, hatchets.

The group was not a usual one. They were not natives seeking work. These had an air of dignity, of quietly following their own purpose. It was the dignity that checked my tongue. I walked quietly on, talking softly to the growling dogs, till I was ten paces away. Then the old man stopped, drawing his blanket close.

''Morning, Nkosikaas,' he said, using the customary greeting for any time of the day.

'Good morning,' I said. 'Where are you going?' My voice was a little truculent.

The old man spoke in his own language, then one of the young men stepped forward politely and said in careful English: 'My Chief travels to see his brothers beyond the river.'

A Chief! I thought, understanding the pride that made the old man stand before me like an equal – more than an equal, for he showed courtesy, and I showed none.

The old man spoke again, wearing dignity like an inherited garment, still standing ten paces off, flanked by his entourage, not looking at me (that would have been rude) but directing his eyes somewhere over my head at the trees.

'You are the little Nkosikaas from the farm of Baas Jordan?'

'That's right,' I said.

'Perhaps your father does not remember,' said the interpreter for the old man, 'but there was an affair with some goats. I remember seeing you when you were . . .' The young man held his hand at knee level and smiled.

We all smiled.

'What is your name?' I asked.

'This is Chief Mshlanga,' said the young man.

'I will tell my father that I met you,' I said.

The old man said: 'My greetings to your father, little Nkosikaas.'

'Good morning,' I said politely, finding the politeness difficult, from lack of use.

"Morning, little Nkosikaas,' said the old man, and stood aside to let me pass.

I went by, my gun hanging awkwardly, the dogs sniffing and growling, cheated of their favourite game of chasing natives like animals.

Not long afterwards I read in an old explorer's book the phrase: 'Chief Mshlanga's country'. It went like this: 'Our destination was Chief Mshlanga's country, to the north of the river; and it was our desire to ask his permission to prospect for gold in his territory.'

The phrase 'ask his permission' was so extraordinary to a white child, brought up to consider all natives as things to use, that it revived those questions, which could not be suppressed: they fermented slowly in my mind.

On another occasion one of those old prospectors who still move over Africa looking for neglected reefs, with their hammers and tents, and pans for sifting gold from crushed rock, came to the farm and, in talking of the old days, used that phrase again: 'This was the Old Chief's country,' he said. 'It stretched from those mountains over there way back to the river, hundreds of miles of country.' That was his name for our district: 'The Old Chief's Country'; he did not use our name for it – a new phrase which held no implication of usurped ownership.

As I read more books about the time when this part of Africa was opened up, not much more than fifty years before, I found Old Chief Mshlanga had been a famous man, known to all the explorers and prospectors. But then he had been young; or maybe it was his father or uncle they spoke of – I never found out.

During that year I met him several times in the part of the farm that was traversed by natives moving over the country. I learned that the path up the side of the big red field where the birds sang was the recognized highway for migrants. Perhaps I even haunted it in the hope of meeting him: being greeted by him, the exchange of courtesies, seemed to answer the questions that troubled me.

Soon I carried a gun in a different spirit; I used it for shooting food and not to give me confidence. And now the dogs learned better manners. When I saw a native approaching, we offered and took greetings; and slowly that other landscape in my mind faded, and my feet struck directly on the African soil, and I saw the shapes of tree and hill clearly, and the black people moved back, as it were, out of my life: it was as if I stood aside to watch a slow intimate dance of landscape and men, a very old dance, whose steps I could not learn.

But I thought: this is my heritage, too; I was bred here; it is my country as well as the black man's country; and there is plenty of room for all of us, without elbowing each other off the pavements and roads.

It seemed it was only necessary to let free that respect I felt when I was talking with old Chief Mshlanga, to let both black and white people meet gently, with tolerance for each other's differences: it seemed quite easy.

Then, one day, something new happened. Working in our house as servants were always three natives: cook, houseboy, garden boy. They used to change as the farm natives changed: stayed for a few months, then moving on to a new job, or back home to their kraals: They were thought of as 'good' or 'bad' natives; which meant: how did they behave as servants? Were they lazy, efficient, obedient, or disrespectful? If the family felt good-humoured, the phrase was: 'What can you expect from raw black savages?' If we were angry, we said: 'These damned niggers, we would be much better off without them.'

One day, a white policeman was on his rounds of the district, and he said laughingly: 'Did you know you have an important man in your kitchen?'

'What!' exclaimed my mother sharply. 'What do you mean?'

'A Chief's son.' The policeman seemed amused. 'He'll boss the tribe when the old man dies.'

'He's better not put on a Chief's son act with me,' said my mother.

When the policeman left, we looked with different eyes at our cook: he was a good worker, but he drank too much at week-ends – that was how we knew him.

He was a tall youth, with very black skin, like black polished metal, his tightly-growing black hair parted white man's fashion at one side, with a metal comb from the store stuck into it; very polite, very distant, very quick to obey an order. Now it had been pointed out, we said: 'Of course, you can see. Blood always tells.'

My mother became strict with him now she knew about his birth and prospects. Sometimes, when she lost her temper, she would say: 'You aren't the Chief yet, you know.' And he would answer her very quietly, his eyes on the ground: 'Yes, Nkosikaas.'

One afternoon he asked for a whole day off, instead of the customary half-day, to go home next Sunday.

'How can you go home in one day?'

'It will take me half an hour on my bicycle,' he explained.

I watched the direction he took; and the next day I went off to look for his kraal; I understood he must be Chief Mshlanga's successor; there was no other kraal near enough our farm.

Beyond our boundaries on that side the country was new to me. I followed unfamiliar paths past kopjes that till now had been part of the jagged horizon, hazed with distance. This was Government land, which had never been cultivated by white men; at first I could not understand why it was that it appeared, in merely crossing the boundary, I had entered a completely fresh type of landscape. It was a wide green valley, where a small river sparkled, and vivid water-birds darted over the rushes. The grass was thick and soft to my calves, the trees stood tall and shapely.

I was used to our farm, whose hundreds of acres of harsh eroded soil bore trees that had been cut for the mine furnaces and had grown thin and twisted, where the cattle had dragged the grass flat, leaving innumerable criss-crossing trails that deepened each season into gullies, under the force of the rains.

This country had been left untouched, save for prospectors whose picks had struck a few sparks from the surface of the rocks as they wandered by; and for migrant natives whose passing had left, perhaps, a charred patch on the trunk of a tree where their evening fire had nestled.

It was very silent: a hot morning with pigeons cooing throatily, the midday shadows lying dense and thick with clear yellow spaces of sunlight between and in all that wide green park-like valley, not a human soul but myself.

I was listening to the quick regular tapping of a woodpecker when slowly a chill feeling seemed to grow up from the small of my back to my shoulders, in a constricting spasm like a shudder, and at the roots of my hair a tingling sensation began and ran down over the surface of my flesh, leaving me goosefleshed and cold, though I was damp with sweat. Fever? I thought; then uneasily, turned to look over my shoulder; and realized suddenly that this was fear. It was extraordinary, even humiliating. It was a new fear. For all the years I had walked by myself over this country I had never known a moment's uneasiness; in the beginning because I had been supported by a gun and the dogs, then because I had learnt an easy friendliness for the natives I might encounter.

I had read of this feeling, how the bigness and silence of Africa, under the ancient sun, grows dense and takes shape in the mind, till even the birds seem to call menacingly, and a deadly spirit comes out of the trees and the rocks. You move warily, as if your very passing disturbs something old and evil, something dark and big and angry that might suddenly rear and strike from behind. You look at groves of entwined trees, and picture the animals that might be lurking there; you look at the river running slowly, dropping from level to level through the vlei, spreading into pools where at night the buck come to drink, and the crocodiles rise and drag them by their soft noses into underwater caves. Fear possessed me. I found I was turning round and round, because of that shapeless menace behind me that might reach out and take me; I kept glancing at the files of kopjes which, seen from a different angle, seemed to change with every step so that even known landmarks, like a big mountain that had sentinelled my world since I first became conscious of it, showed an unfamiliar sunlit valley among its foothills. I did not know where I was. I was lost. Panic seized me. I found I was spinning round and round, staring anxiously at this tree and that, peering up at the sun which appeared to have moved into an eastern slant, shedding the sad yellow light of sunset. Hours must have passed! I looked at my watch and found that this state of meaningless terror had lasted perhaps ten minutes.

The point was that it was meaningless. I was not ten miles from home: I had only to take my way back along the valley to find myself at the fence: away among the foothills of the kopjes gleamed the roof of a neighbour's house, and a couple of hours' walking would reach it. This was the sort of fear that contracts the flesh of a dog at night and sets him howling at the full moon. It had nothing to do with what I thought or felt: and I was more disturbed by the fact that I could become its victim than of the physical sensation itself: I walked steadily on, quietened, in a divided mind, watching my own pricking nerves and apprehensive glances from side to side with a disgusted amusement. Deliberately I set myself to think of this village I was seeking, and what I should do when I entered it – if I could find it, which was doubtful, since I was walking aimlessly and it might be anywhere in the hundreds of thousands of acres of bush that stretched about me. With my mind on that village, I realized that a new sensation was added to the fear: loneliness. Now such a terror of isolation invaded me that I could hardly walk; and if it were not that I came over the crest of a small rise and saw a village below me, I should have turned and gone home. It was a cluster of thatched huts in a clearing among trees. There were neat patches of mealies and pumpkins and millet, and cattle grazed under some trees at a distance. Fowls scratched among the huts, dogs lay sleeping on the grass, and goats friezed a kopje that jutted up beyond a tributary of the river lying like an enclosing arm round the village.

As I came close I saw the huts were lovingly decorated with patterns of yellow and red and ochre mud on the walls; and the thatch was tied in place with plaits of straw.

This was not at all like our farm compound, a dirty and neglected place, a temporary home for migrants who had no roots in it.

And now I did not know what to do next. I called a small black boy, who was sitting on a log playing a stringed gourd, quite naked except for the strings of blue beads round his neck, and said: 'Tell the Chief I am here.' The child stuck his thumb in his mouth and stared shyly back at me.

For minutes I shifted my feet on the edge of what seemed a deserted village, till at last the child scuttled off, and then some women came. They were draped in bright cloths, with brass glinting in their ears and on their arms. They also stared, silently; then turned to chatter among themselves.

I said again: 'Can I see Chief Mshlanga?' I saw they caught the name; they did not understand what I wanted. I did not understand myself.

At last I walked through them and came past the huts and saw a clearing under a big shady tree, where a dozen old men sat cross-legged on the ground, talking. Chief Mshlanga was leaning back against the tree, holding a gourd in his hand, from which he had been drinking. When he saw me, not a muscle of his face moved, and I could see he was not pleased: perhaps he was afflicted with my own shyness, due to being unable to find the right forms of courtesy for the occasion. To meet me, on our own farm, was one thing; but I should not have come here. What had I expected? I could not join them socially: the thing was unheard of. Bad enough that I, a white girl, should be walking the veld alone as a white man might: and in this part of the bush where only Government officials had the right to move.

Again I stood, smiling foolishly, while behind me stood the groups of brightly-clad, chattering women, their faces alert with curiosity and interest, and in front of me sat the old men, with old lined faces, their eyes guarded, aloof. It was a village of ancients and children and women. Even the two young men who kneeled beside the Chief were not those I had seen with him previously: the young men were all away working on the white men's farms and mines, and the Chief must depend on relatives who were temporarily on holiday for his attendants.

'The small white Nkosikaas is far from home,' remarked the old man at last.

'Yes,' I agreed, 'it is far.' I wanted to say: 'I have come to pay you a friendly visit, Chief Mshlanga.' I could not say it. I might now be feeling an urgent helpless desire to get to know these men and women as people, to be accepted by them as a friend, but the truth was I had set out in a spirit of curiosity: I had wanted to see the village that our cook, the reserved and obedient young man who got drunk on Sundays, would one day rule over.

'The child of Nkosi Jordan is welcome,' said Chief Mshlanga.

'Thank you,' I said, and could think of nothing more to say. There was a silence, while the flies rose and began to buzz around my head; and the wind shook a little in the thick green tree that spread its branches over the old men.

'Good morning,' I said at last. 'I have to return now to my home.'

''Morning, little Nkosikaas,' said Chief Mshlanga.

I walked away from the indifferent village, over the rise past the staring amber-eyed goats, down through the tall stately trees into the great rich green valley where the river meandered and the pigeons cooed tales of plenty and the woodpecker tapped softly.

The fear had gone; the loneliness had set into stiff-necked stoicism; there was now a queer hostility in the landscape, a cold, hard, sullen indomitability that walked with me, as strong as a wall, as intangible as smoke; it seemed to say to me: you walk here as a destroyer. I went slowly homewards, with an empty heart: I had learned that if one cannot call a country to heel like a dog, neither can one dismiss the past with a smile in an easy gush of feeling, saying: I could not help it, I am also a victim.

I only saw Chief Mshlanga once again.

One night my father's big red land was trampled down by small sharp hooves, and it was discovered that the culprits were goats from Chief Mshlanga's kraal. This had happened once before, years ago.

My father confiscated all the goats. Then he sent a message to the old Chief that if he wanted them he would have to pay for the damage.

He arrived at our house at the time of sunset one evening, looking very old and bent now, walking stiffly under his regally-draped blanket, leaning on a big stick. My father sat himself down in his big chair below the steps of the house; the old man squatted carefully on the ground before him, flanked by his two young men.

The palaver was long and painful, because of the bad English of the young man who interpreted, and because my father could not speak dialect, but only kitchen kaffir.

From my father's point of view, at least two hundred pounds' worth of damage had been done to the crop. He knew he could not get the money from the old man. He felt he was entitled to keep the goats. As for the old Chief, he kept repeating angrily: 'Twenty goats! My people cannot lose twenty goats! We are not rich, like the Nkosi Jordan, to lose twenty goats at once.'

My father did not think of himself as rich, but rather as very poor. He spoke quickly and angrily in return, saying that the damage done meant a great deal to him, and that he was entitled to the goats.

At last it grew so heated that the cook, the Chief's son, was called from the kitchen to be interpreter, and now my father spoke fluently in English, and our cook translated rapidly so that the old man could understand how very angry my father was. The young man spoke without emotion, in a mechanical way, his eyes lowered, but showing how he felt his position by a hostile uncomfortable set of the shoulders.

It was now in the late sunset, the sky a welter of colours, the birds singing their last songs, and the cattle, lowing peacefully, moving past us towards their sheds for the night. It was the hour when Africa is most beautiful; and here was this pathetic, ugly scene, doing no one any good.

At last my father stated finally: 'I'm not going to argue about it. I am keeping the goats.'

The old Chief flashed back in his own language: 'That means that my people will go hungry when the dry season comes.'

'Go to the police, then,' said my father, and looked triumphant.

There was, of course, no more to be said.

The old man sat silent, his head bent, his hands dangling helplessly over his withered knees. Then he rose, the young man helping him, and he stood facing my father. He spoke once again, very stiffly; and turned away and went home to his village.

'What did he say?' asked my father of the young man, who laughed uncomfortably and would not meet his eyes.

'What did he say?' insisted my father.

Our cook stood straight and silent, his brows knotted together. Then he spoke. 'My father says: All this land, this land you call yours, is his land and belongs to our people.'

Having made this statement, he walked off into the bush after his father, and we did not see him again.

Our next cook was a migrant from Nyasaland, with no expectations of greatness.

Next time the policeman came on his rounds he was told this story. He remarked: 'That kraal has no right to be there; it should have been moved long ago. I don't know why no one has done anything about it. I'll have a chat to the Native Commissioner next week. I'm going over for tennis on Sunday, anyway.'

Some time later we heard that Chief Mshlanga and his people had been moved two hundred miles east, to a proper native reserve; the Government land was going to be opened up for white settlement soon.

I went to see the village again, about a year afterwards. There was nothing there. Mounds of red mud, where the huts had been, had long swathes of rotting thatch over them, veined with the red galleries of the white ants. The pumpkin vines rioted everywhere, over the bushes, up the lower branches of trees so that the great golden balls rolled underfoot and dangled overhead: it was a festival of pumpkins. The bushes were crowding up, the new grass sprang vivid green.

The settler lucky enough to be alloted the lush warm valley (if he chose to cultivate this particular section) would find, suddenly, in the middle of a mealie field, the plants were growing fifteen feet tall, the weight of the cobs dragging at the stalks, and wonder what unsuspected vein of richness he had struck.

A Sunrise on the Veld

Every night that winter he said aloud into the dark of the pillow:
Half-past four! Half-past four! till he felt his brain had gripped
the words and held them fast. Then he fell asleep at once, as if a
shutter had fallen; and lay with his face turned to the clock so
that he could see it first thing when he woke.

It was half-past four to the minute, every morning. Trium-
phantly pressing down the alarm-knob of the clock, which the
dark half of his mind had outwitted, remaining vigilant all night
and counting the hours as he lay relaxed in sleep, he huddled
down for a last warm moment under the clothes, playing with
the idea of lying abed for this once only. But he played with it for
the fun of knowing that it was a weakness he could defeat without
effort; just as he set the alarm each night for the delight of the
moment when he woke and stretched his limbs, feeling the
muscles tighten, and thought: Even my brain – even that! I can
control every part of myself.

Luxury of warm rested body, with the arms and legs and
fingers waiting like soldiers for a word of command! Joy of
knowing that the precious hours were given to sleep voluntarily!
– for he had once stayed awake three nights running, to prove
that he could, and then worked all day, refusing even to admit
that he was tired; and now sleep seemed to him a servant to be
commanded and refused.

The boy stretched his frame full-length, touching the wall at
his head with his hands, and the bedfoot with his toes; then he
sprang out, like a fish leaping from water. And it was cold, cold.

He always dressed rapidly, so as to try and conserve his night-
warmth till the sun rose two hours later; but by the time he had
on his clothes his hands were numbed and he could scarcely hold

his shoes. These he could not put on for fear of waking his parents, who never came to know how early he rose.

As soon as he stepped over the lintel, the flesh of his soles contracted on the chilled earth, and his legs began to ache with cold. It was night; the stars were glittering, the trees standing black and still. He looked for signs of day, for the greying of the edge of a stone, or a lightening in the sky where the sun would rise, but there was nothing yet. Alert as an animal he crept past the dangerous window, standing poised with his hand on the sill for one proudly fastidious moment, looking in at the stuffy blackness of the room where his parents lay.

Feeling for the grass-edge of the path with his toes, he reached inside another window further along the wall, where his gun had been set in readiness the night before. The steel was icy, and numbed fingers slipped along it, so that he had to hold it in the crook of his arm for safety. Then he tiptoed to the room where the dogs slept, and was fearful that they might have been tempted to go before him; but they were waiting, their haunches crouched in reluctance at the cold, but ears and swinging tails greeting the gun ecstatically. His warning undertone kept them secret and silent till the house was a hundred yards back: then they bolted off into the bush, yelping excitedly. The boy imagined his parents turning in their beds and muttering: Those dogs again! before they were dragged back in sleep; and he smiled scornfully. He always looked back over his shoulder at the house before he passed a wall of trees that shut it from sight. It looked so low and small, crouching there under a tall and brilliant sky. Then he turned his back on it, and on the frowsting sleepers, and forgot them.

He would have to hurry. Before the light grew strong he must be four miles away; and already a tint of green stood in the hollow of a leaf, and the air smelled of morning and the stars were dimming.

He slung the shoes over his shoulder, veld skoen that were crinkled and hard with the dews of a hundred mornings. They would be necessary when the ground became too hot to bear. Now he felt the chilled dust push up between his toes, and he let the muscles of his feet spread and settle into the shapes of the earth; and he thought: I could walk a hundred miles on feet like these! I could walk all day, and never tire!

He was walking swiftly through the dark tunnel of foliage that in daytime was a road. The dogs were invisibly ranging the lower travelways of the bush, and he heard them panting. Sometimes he felt a cold muzzle on his leg before they were off again, scouting for a trail to follow. They were not trained, but free-running companions of the hunt, who often tired of the long stalk before the final shots, and went off on their own pleasure. Soon he could see them, small and wild-looking in a wild strange light, now that the bush stood trembling on the verge of colour, waiting for the sun to paint earth and grass afresh.

The grass stood to his shoulders; and the trees were showering a faint silvery rain. He was soaked; his whole body was clenched in a steady shiver.

Once he bent to the road that was newly scored with animal trails, and regretfully straightened, reminding himself that the pleasure of tracking must wait till another day.

He began to run along the edge of a field, noting jerkily how it was filmed over with fresh spiderweb, so that the long reaches of great black clods seemed netted in glistening grey. He was using the steady lope he had learned by watching the natives, the run that is a dropping of the weight of the body from one foot to the next in a slow balancing movement that never tires, nor shortens the breath; and he felt the blood pulsing down his legs and along his arms, and the exultation and pride of body mounted in him till he was shutting his teeth hard against a violent desire to shout his triumph.

Soon he had left the cultivated part of the farm. Behind him the bush was low and black. In front was a long vlei, acres of long pale grass that sent back a hollowing gleam of light to a satiny sky. Near him thick swathes of grass were bent with the weight of water, and diamond drops sparkled on each frond.

The first bird woke at his feet and at once a flock of them sprang into the air calling shrilly that day had come; and suddenly, behind him, the bush woke into song, and he could hear the guinea-fowl calling far ahead of him. That meant they would now be sailing down from their trees into thick grass, and it was for them he had come: he was too late. But he did not mind. He forgot he had come to shoot. He set his legs wide, and balanced from foot to foot, and swung his gun up and down in both hands horizontally, in a kind of improvised exercise, and let his head sink back till it was pillowed in his neck muscles, and watched how above him small rosy clouds floated in a lake of gold.

Suddenly, it all rose in him; it was unbearable. He leapt into the air, shouting and yelling wild, unrecognizable noises. Then he began to run, not carefully, as he had before, but madly, like a wild thing. He was clean crazy, yelling mad with the joy of living and a superfluity of youth. He rushed down the vlei under a tumult of crimson and gold, while all the birds of the world sang about him. He ran in great leaping strides, and shouted as he ran, feeling his body rise into the crisp rushing air and fall back surely on to sure feet; and thought briefly, not believing that such a thing could happen to him that he could break his ankle any moment, in this thick tangled grass. He cleared bushes like a duiker, leaped over rocks; and finally came to a dead stop at a place where the ground fell abruptly away below him to the river. It had been a two-mile-long dash through waist-high growth, and he was breathing hoarsely and could no longer sing. But he poised on a rock and looked down at stretches of water that gleamed through stooping trees, and thought suddenly, I am fifteen! Fifteen! The words came new to him; so that he kept repeating them wonderingly, with swelling excitement; and he felt the years of his life with his hands, as it were, as if he were counting marbles, each one hard and separate and compact, each one a wonderful shining thing. That was what he was: fifteen years of this rich soil, and this slow-moving water, and air that smelt like a challenge whether it was warm and sultry at noon, or as brisk as cold water, like it was now.

There was nothing he couldn't do, nothing! A vision came to him, as he stood there, like when a child hears the word 'eternity' and tries to understand it, and time takes possession of the mind. He felt his life ahead of him as a great and wonderful thing, something that was his; and he said aloud, with the blood rising to his head: all the great men of the world have been as I am now, and there is nothing I can't become, nothing I can't do; there is no country in the world I cannot make part of myself, if

I choose. I contain the world. I can make of it what I want. If I choose, I can change everything that is going to happen: it depends on me, and what I decide now.

The urgency, and the truth and the courage of what his voice was saying exulted him so that he began to sing again, at the top of his voice, and the sound went echoing down the river gorge. He stopped for the echo, and sang again: stopped and shouted. That was what he was! – he sang, if he chose; and the world had to answer him.

And for minutes he stood there, shouting and singing and waiting for the lovely eddying sound of the echo; so that his own new strong thoughts came back and washed round his head, as if someone were answering him and encouraging him; till the gorge was full of soft voices clashing back and forth from rock to rock over the river. And then it seemed as if there was a new voice. He listened, puzzled, for it was not his own. Soon he was leaning forward, all his nerves alert, quite still: somewhere close to him there was a noise that was no joyful bird, nor tinkle of falling water, nor ponderous movement of cattle.

There it was again. In the deep morning hush that held his future and his past, was a sound of pain, and repeated over and over: it was a kind of shortened scream, as if someone, something, had no breath to scream. He came to himself, looked about him, and called for the dogs. They did not appear: they had gone off on their own business, and he was alone. Now he was clean sober, all the madness gone. His heart beating fast, because of that frightened screaming, he stepped carefully off the rock and went towards a belt of trees. He was moving cautiously, for not so long ago he had seen a leopard in just this spot.

At the edge of the trees he stopped and peered, holding his gun ready; he advanced, looking steadily about him, his eyes narrowed. Then, all at once, in the middle of a step, he faltered, and his face was puzzled. He shook his head impatiently, as if he doubted his own sight.

There, between two rocks, against a background of gaunt black rocks, was a figure from a dream, a strange beast that was horned and drunken-legged, but like something he had never even imagined. It seemed to be ragged. It looked like a small buck that had black ragged tufts of fur standing up irregularly all over it, with patches of raw flesh beneath . . . but the patches of rawness were disappearing under moving black and came again elsewhere; and all the time the creature screamed, in small gasping screams, and leaped drunkenly from side to side, as if it were blind.

Then the boy understood: it *was* a buck. He ran closer, and again stood still, stopped by a new fear. Around him the grass was whispering and alive. He looked wildly about, and then down. The ground was black with ants, great energetic ants that took no notice of him, but hurried and scurried towards the fighting shape, like glistening black water flowing through the grass.

And, as he drew in his breath and pity and terror seized him, the beast fell and the screaming stopped. Now he could hear nothing but one bird singing, and the sound of the rustling, whispering ants.

He peered over at the writhing blackness that jerked convulsively with the jerking nerves. It grew quieter. There were small twitches from the mass that still looked vaguely like the shape of a small animal.

It came into his mind that he should shoot it and end its pain; and he raised the gun. Then he lowered it again. The buck could no longer feel; its fighting was a mechanical protest of the nerves. But it was not that that made him put down the gun. It was a swelling feeling of rage and misery and protest that expressed itself in the thought: if I had not come it would have died like this: so why should I interfere? All over the bush things like this happen; they happen all the time; this is how life goes on, by living things dying in anguish. He gripped the gun between his knees and felt in his own limbs the myriad swarming pain of the twitching animal that could no longer feel, and set his teeth, and said over and over again under his breath: I can't stop it, I can't stop it. There is nothing I can do.

He was glad that the buck was unconscious and had gone past suffering so that he did not have to make a decision to kill it even when he was feeling with his whole body: this is what happens, this is how things work.

It was right – that was what he was feeling. *It was right and nothing could alter it.*

The knowledge of fatality, of what has to be, had gripped him and for the first time in his life; and he was left unable to make any movement of brain or body, except to say: 'Yes, yes. That is what living is.' It had entered his flesh and his bones and grown in to the furthest corners of his brain and would never leave him. And at that moment he could not have performed the smallest action of mercy, knowing as he did, having lived on it all his life, the vast unalterable, cruel veld, where at any moment one might stumble over a skull or crush the skeleton of some small creature.

Suffering, sick, and angry, but also grimly satisfied with his new stoicism, he stood there leaning on his rifle, and watched the seething black mound grow smaller. At his feet, now, were ants trickling back with pink fragments in their mouths, and there was a fresh acid smell in his nostrils. He sternly controlled the uselessly convulsing muscles of his empty stomach, and reminded himself: the ants must eat too! At the same time he found that the tears were streaming down his face, and his clothes were soaked with the sweat of that other creature's pain.

The shape had grown small. Now it looked like nothing recognizable. He did not know how long it was before he saw the blackness thin, and bits of white showed through, shining in the sun – yes, there was the sun, just up, glowing over the rocks. Why, the whole thing could not have taken longer than a few minutes.

He began to swear, as if the shortness of the time was in itself unbearable, using the words he had heard his father say. He strode forward, crushing ants with each step, and brushing them off his clothes, till he stood above the skeleton, which lay sprawled under a small bush. It was clean-picked. It might have been lying there years, save that on the white bones were pink fragments of gristle. About the bones ants were ebbing away, their pincers full of meat.

The boy looked at them, big black ugly insects. A few were standing and gazing up at him with small glittering eyes.

'Go away!' he said to the ants, very coldly. 'I am not for you – not just yet, at any rate. Go away.' And he fancied that the ants turned and went away.

He bent over the bones and touched the sockets in the skull; that was where the eyes were, he thought incredulously, remembering the liquid dark eyes of a buck. And then he bent the slim foreleg bone, swinging it horizontally in his palm.

That morning, perhaps an hour ago, this small creature had been stepping proud and free through the bush, feeling the chill on its hide even as he himself had done, exhilarated by it. Proudly stepping the earth, tossing its horns, frisking a pretty white tail, it had sniffed the cold morning air. Walking like kings and conquerors it had moved through this free-held bush, where each blade of grass grew for it alone, and where the river ran pure sparkling water for its slaking.

And then – what had happened? Such a swift surefooted thing could surely not be trapped by a swarm of ants?

The boy bent curiously to the skeleton. Then he saw that the back leg that lay uppermost and strained out in the tension of death, was snapped midway in the thigh, so that broken bones jutted over each other uselessly. So that was it! Limping into the ant-masses it could not escape, once it had sensed the danger. Yes, but how had the leg been broken? Had it fallen, perhaps? Impossible, a buck was too light and graceful. Had some jealous rival horned it?

What could possibly have happened? Perhaps some natives had thrown stones at it, as they do, trying to kill it for meat, and had broken its leg. Yes, that must be it.

Even as he imagined the crowd of running, shouting natives, and the flying stones, and the leaping buck, another picture came into his mind. He saw himself, on any one of these bright ringing mornings, drunk with excitement, taking a snap-shot at some half-seen buck. He saw himself, with the gun lowered, wondering whether he had missed or not; and thinking at last that it was late, and he wanted his breakfast, and it was not worth while to track miles after an animal that would very likely get away from him in any case.

For a moment he would not face it. He was a small boy again, kicking sulkily at the skeleton, hanging his head, refusing to accept the responsibility.

Then he straightened up, and looked down at the bones with an odd expression of dismay, all the anger gone out of him. His mind went quite empty: all around him he could see trickles of ants disappearing into the grass. The whispering noise was faint and dry, like the rustling of a cast snakeskin.

At last he picked up his gun and walked homewards. He was

telling himself half defiantly that he wanted his breakfast. He was telling himself that it was getting very hot, much too hot to be out roaming the bush.

Really, he was tired. He walked heavily, not looking where he put his feet. When he came within sight of his home he stopped, knitted his brows. There was something he had to think out. The death of that small animal was a thing that concerned him, and he was by no means finished with it. It lay at the back of his mind uncomfortably.

Soon, the very next morning, he would get clear of everybody and go to the bush and think about it.

No Witchcraft for Sale

The Farquars had been childless for years when little Teddy was born; and they were touched by the pleasure of their servants, who brought presents of fowls and eggs and flowers to the homestead when they came to rejoice over the baby, exclaiming with delight over his downy golden head and his blue eyes. They congratulated Mrs Farquar as if she had achieved a very great thing, and she felt that she had – her smile for the lingering, admiring natives was warm and grateful.

Later, when Teddy had his first haircut, Gideon the cook picked up the soft gold tufts from the ground, and held them reverently in his hand. Then he smiled at the little boy and said: 'Little Yellow Head'. That became the native name for the child. Gideon and Teddy were great friends from the first. When Gideon had finished his work, he would lift Teddy on his shoulders to the shade of a big tree, and play with him there, forming curious little toys from twigs and leaves and grass, or shaping animals from wetted soil. When Teddy learned to walk it was often Gideon who crouched before him, clucking encouragement, finally catching him when he fell, tossing him up in the air till they both became breathless with laughter. Mrs Farquar was fond of the old cook because of his love for her child.

There was no second baby; and one day Gideon said: 'Ah, missus, missus, the Lord above sent this one; Little Yellow Head is the most good thing we have in our house.' Because of that 'we' Mrs Farquar felt a warm impulse towards her cook; and at the end of the month she raised his wages. He had been with her now for several years; he was one of the few natives who had his wife and children in the compound and never wanted to go home to his kraal, which was some hundreds of miles away. Sometimes a small piccanin who had been born the same time as Teddy, could be seen peering from the edge of the bush, staring in awe at the little white boy with his miraculous fair hair and northern blue eyes. The two little children would gaze at each other with a wide, interested gaze, and once Teddy put out his hand curiously to touch the black child's cheeks and hair.

Gideon, who was watching, shook his head wonderingly, and said: 'Ah, missus, these are both children, and one will grow up to be a Baas, and one will be a servant'; and Mrs Farquar smiled and said sadly, 'Yes, Gideon, I was thinking the same.' She sighed. 'It is God's will,' said Gideon, who was a mission boy. The Farquars were very religious people; and this shared feeling about God bound servant and masters even closer together.

Teddy was about six years old when he was given a scooter, and discovered the intoxications of speed. All day he would fly around the homestead, in and out of flowerbeds, scattering squawking chickens and irritated dogs, finishing with a wide dizzying arc into the kitchen door. Then he would cry: 'Gideon, look at me!' And Gideon would laugh and say: 'Very clever, Little Yellow Head.' Gideon's youngest son, who was now a herdsboy, came especially up from the compound to see the scooter. He was afraid to come near it, but Teddy showed off in front of him. 'Piccanin,' shouted Teddy, 'get out of my way!' And he raced in circles around the black child until he was frightened, and fled back to the bush.

'Why did you frighten him?' asked Gideon, gravely reproachful.

Teddy said defiantly: 'He's only a black boy,' and laughed. Then, when Gideon turned away from him without speaking, his face fell. Very soon he slipped into the house and found an orange and brought it to Gideon, saying: 'This is for you.' He could not bring himself to say he was sorry; but he could not bear to lose Gideon's affection either. Gideon took the orange unwillingly and sighed. 'Soon you will be going away to school, Little Yellow Head,' he said wonderingly, 'and then you will be grown up.' He shook his head gently and said, 'And that is how our lives go.' He seemed to be putting a distance between himself and Teddy, not because of resentment, but in the way a person accepts something inevitable. The baby had lain in his arms and smiled up into his face: the tiny boy had swung from his shoulders, had played with him by the hour. Now Gideon would not let his flesh touch the flesh of the white child. He was kind, but there was a grave formality in his voice that made Teddy pout and sulk away. Also it made him into a man: with Gideon he was polite, and carried himself formally, and if he came into the kitchen to ask for something, it was in the way a white man uses towards a servant, expecting to be obeyed.

But on the day that Teddy came staggering into the kitchen with his fists to his eyes, shrieking with pain, Gideon dropped the pot full of hot soup that he was holding, rushed to the child, and forced aside his fingers. 'A snake!' he exclaimed. Teddy had been on his scooter, and had come to a rest with his foot on the side of a big tub of plants. A tree snake, hanging by its tail from the roof, had spat full into his eyes. Mrs Farquar came running when she heard the commotion. 'He'll go blind,' she sobbed, holding Teddy close against her. 'Gideon, he'll go blind!' Already the eyes, with perhaps half an hour's sight left in them, were swollen up to the size of fists: Teddy's small white face was distorted by great purple oozing protuberances. Gideon said: 'Wait a minute, missus, I'll get some medicine.' He ran off into the bush.

Mrs Farquar lifted the child into the house and bathed his eyes with permanganate. She had scarcely heard Gideon's words; but when she saw that her remedies had no effect at all, and remembered how she had seen natives with no sight in their eyes, because of the spitting of a snake, she began to look for the return of her cook, remembering what she had heard of the efficacy of native herbs. She stood by the window, holding the terrified, sobbing little boy in her arms, and peered helplessly into the bush. It was not more than a few minutes before she saw Gideon come bounding back, and in his hand he held a plant.

'Do not be afraid, missus,' said Gideon, 'this will cure Little Yellow Head's eyes.' He stripped the leaves from the plant, leaving a small white flesh root. Without even washing it he put the root in his mouth, chewed it vigorously, and then held the spittle there while he took the child forcibly from Mrs Farquar. He gripped Teddy down between his knees, and pressed the balls of his thumbs into the swollen eyes, so that the child screamed and Mrs Farquar cried out in protest: 'Gideon! Gideon!' But

Gideon took no notice. He knelt over the writhing child, pushing back the puffy lids till chinks of eyeball showed, and then he spat hard, again and again, into first one eye, and then the other. He finally lifted Teddy gently into his mother's arms, and said: 'His eyes will get better.' But Mrs Farquar was weeping with terror, and she could hardly thank him: it was impossible to believe that Teddy could keep his sight. In a couple of hours the swellings were gone; the eyes were inflamed and tender but Teddy could see. Mr and Mrs Farquar went to Gideon in the kitchen and thanked him over and over again. They felt helpless because of their gratitude: it seemed they could do nothing to express it. They gave Gideon presents for his wife and children, and a big increase in wages, but these things could not pay for Teddy's now completely cured eyes. Mrs Farquar said: 'Gideon, God chose you as an instrument for His goodness,' and Gideon said: 'Yes, missus, God is very good.'

Now, when such a thing happens on a farm, it cannot be long before everyone hears of it. Mr and Mrs Farquar told their neighbours and the story was discussed from one end of the district to the other. The bush is full of secrets. No one can live in Africa, or at least on the veld, without learning very soon that there is an ancient wisdom of leaf and soil and season – and, too, perhaps most important of all, of the darker tracts of the human mind – which is the black man's heritage. Up and down the district people were telling anecdotes, reminding each other of things that had happened to them.

'But I saw it myself, I tell you. It was a puff-adder bite. The kaffir's arm was swollen to the elbow, like a great shiny black bladder. He was groggy after half a minute. He was dying. Then suddenly a kaffir walked out of the bush with his hands full of green stuff. He smeared something on the place, and next day my boy was back at work, and all you could see was two small punctures in the skin.'

This was the kind of tale they told. And, as always, with a certain amount of exasperation, because while all of them knew that in the bush of Africa are waiting valuable drugs locked in bark, in simple-looking leaves, in roots, it was impossible to ever get the truth about them from the natives themselves.

The story eventually reached town; and perhaps it was at a

sundowner party, or some such function, that a doctor who happened to be there challenged it. 'Nonsense,' he said. 'These things get exaggerated in the telling. We are always checking up on this kind of story, and we draw a blank every time.'

Anyway, one morning there arrived a strange car at the homestead, and out stepped one of the workers from the laboratory in town, with cases full of test-tubes and chemicals.

Mr and Mrs Farquar were flustered and pleased and flattered. They asked the scientist to lunch, and they told the story all over again, for the hundredth time. Little Teddy was there too, his blue eyes sparkling with health, to prove the truth of it. The scientist explained how humanity might benefit if this new drug could be offered for sale, and the Farquars were even more pleased; they were kind, simple people, who liked to think of something good coming about because of them. But when the scientist began talking of the money that might result, their manner showed discomfort. Their feelings over the miracle (that was how they thought of it) were so strong and deep and religious, that it was distasteful to them to think of money. The scientist, seeing their faces, went back to his first point, which was the advancement of humanity. He was perhaps a trifle perfunctory: it was not the first time he had come salting the tail of a fabulous bush-secret.

Eventually, when the meal was over, the Farquars called Gideon into their living-room and explained to him that this baas, here, was a Big Doctor from the Big City, and he had come all that way to see Gideon. At this Gideon seemed afraid; he did not understand; and Mrs Farquar explained quickly that it was because of the wonderful thing he had done with Teddy's eyes that the Big Baas had come.

Giden looked from Mrs Farquar to Mr Farquar, and then at the little boy, who was showing great importance because of the occasion. At last he said grudgingly: 'The Big Baas wants to know what medicine I used?' He spoke incredulously, as if he could not believe his old friends could so betray him. Mr Farquar began explaining how a useful medicine could be made out of the root, and how it could be put on sale, and how thousands of people, black and white, up and down the continent of Africa, could be saved by the medicine when that spitting snake filled their eyes with poison. Gideon listened, his eyes bent on the ground, the skin of his forehead puckering in discomfort. When Mr Farquar had finished he did not reply. The scientist, who all this time had been leaning back in a big chair, sipping his coffee and smiling with sceptical good-humour, chipped in and explained all over again, in different words, about the making of drugs and the progress of science. Also, he offered Gideon a present.

There was silence after this further explanation, and then Gideon remarked indifferently that he could not remember the root. His face was sullen and hostile, even when he looked at the Farquars, whom he usually treated like old friends. They were beginning to feel annoyed; and this feeling annulled the guilt that had been sprung into life by Gideon's accusing manner. They were beginning to feel that he was unreasonable. But it was at that moment that they all realized he would never give in. The magical drug would remain where it was, unknown and useless except for the tiny scattering of Africans who had the knowledge, natives who might be digging a ditch for the municipality in a ragged shirt and a pair of patched shorts, but who were still born to healing, hereditary healers, being the nephews or sons of the old witch doctors whose ugly masks and bits of bone and all the uncouth properties of magic were the outward signs of real power and wisdom.

The Farquars might tread on that plant fifty times a day as they passed from house to garden, from cow kraal to mealie field, but they would never know it.

But they went on persuading and arguing, with all the force of their exasperation; and Gideon continued to say that he could not remember, or that there was no such root, or that it was the wrong season of the year, or that it wasn't the root itself, but the spittle from his mouth that had cured Teddy's eyes. He said all these things one after another, and seemed not to care they were contradictory. He was rude and stubborn. The Farquars could hardly recognize their gentle, lovable old servant in this ignorant, perversely obstinate native, standing there in front of them with lowered eyes, his hands twitching his cook's apron, repeating over and over whichever one of the stupid refusals that first entered his head.

And suddenly he appeared to give in. He lifted his head, gave a long, blank angry look at the circle of whites, who seemed to him like a circle of yelping dogs pressing around him, and said: 'I will show you the root.'

They walked single file away from the homestead down a kaffir path. It was a blazing December afternoon, with the sky full of hot rain-clouds. Everything was hot: the sun was like a bronze tray whirling overhead, there was a heat shimmer over the fields, the soil was scorching underfoot, the dusty wind blew gritty and thick and warm in their faces. It was a terrible day, fit only for reclining on a verandah with iced drinks, which is where they would normally have been at that hour.

From time to time, remembering that on the day of the snake it had taken ten minutes to find the root, someone asked: 'Is it much further, Gideon?' And Gideon would answer over his shoulder, with angry politeness: 'I'm looking for the root, baas.' And indeed, he would frequently bend sideways and trail his hand among the grasses with a gesture that was insulting in its perfunctoriness. He walked them through the bush along unknown paths for two hours, in that melting destroying heat, so that the sweat trickled coldly down them and their heads ached. They were all quite silent: the Farquars because they were angry, the scientist because he was being proved right again; there was no such plant. His was a tactful silence.

At last, six miles from the house, Gideon suddenly decided they had had enough; or perhaps his anger evaporated at that moment. He picked up, without any attempt at looking anything but casual, a handful of blue flowers from the grass, flowers that had been growing plentifully all down the paths they had come.

He handed them to the scientist without looking at him, and marched off by himself on the way home, leaving them to follow him if they chose.

When they got back to the house, the scientist went to the kitchen to thank Gideon: he was being very polite, even though there was an amused look in his eyes. Gideon was not there. Throwing the flowers casually into the back of his car, the eminent visitor departed on his way back to his laboratory.

Gideon was back in his kitchen in time to prepare dinner, but he was sulking. He spoke to Mrs Farquar like an unwilling servant. It was days before they liked each other again.

The Farquars made enquiries about the root from their labourers. Sometimes they were answered with distrustful stares. Sometimes the natives said: 'We do not know. We have never heard of the root.' One, the cattle boy, who had been with them a long time and had grown to trust them a little, said: 'Ask your boy in the kitchen. Now, there's a doctor for you. He's the son of a famous medicine man who used to be in these parts, and there's nothing he cannot cure.' Then he added politely: 'Of course, he's not as good as the white man's doctor, we know that, but he's good for us.'

After some time, when the soreness had gone from between the Farquars and Gideon, they began to joke: 'When are you going to show us the snake-root, Gideon?' and he would laugh and shake his head, saying, a little uncomfortably: 'But I did show you, missus, have you forgotten?'

Much later, Teddy, as a schoolboy, would come into the kitchen and say: 'You old rascal, Gideon! Do you remember the time you tricked us all by making us walk miles all over the veld for nothing? It was so far my father had to carry me!'

And Gideon would double up with polite laughter. After much laughing, he would suddenly straighten himself up, wipe his old eyes, and look sadly at Teddy, who was grinning mischievously at him across the kitchen: 'Ah, Little Yellow Head, how you have grown! Soon you will be grown up with a farm of your own . . .'